HER MAFIA KING
KNIGHT MAFIA TRILOGY

VIOLET PAIGE

PART ONE

CHAPTER 1

KNIGHT

O rgan music. Fucking organ music filled the air, accompanied by the church choir in the loft behind our heads. I adjusted one cufflink and then the other. I wasn't known to stall, but what kind of person was eager to give a eulogy? Especially when that man was the devil.

Uncle Zeke.

I cleared my throat. My aunt clutched my hand with an ice-like grip before I stood from the pew. There was something desperate and pleading in her eyes. I leaned down to peck her check, only because I knew everyone was watching.

"Don't worry. I won't destroy my own name," I whispered.

With that, she seemed to relax into her seat, no longer needing the assurance of my father or sister, planted on either side of her.

With the notes tucked in my breast pocket I took my position in the pulpit—a space I never wanted to command. Death had tapped me for this moment. There was little I could do to say no. Not as Zeke's only nephew. The man didn't have children. There were no other heirs. I looked out on the congregation gathered to pay their social respects to this man. Their expressions vapid. Eyes tearless. I wondered who in this church was responsible for my uncle's murder.

"Thank you. My Uncle Zeke would have been warmed to see so many family and friends gathered here today to say goodbye." My voice carried, assisted by the microphone. I scanned each pew, each bowed head, each set of hands fumbling with a rosary. They were all suspects.

But the truth was, in this congregation no one was truly ever innocent. If they ever confessed the sins on their tongues would spill over the confessional and drain into the sewers and catacombs beneath the cathedral. There was enough to drown the city in this one building.

By the time I finished, Father Philip was ready to usher me off his territory. I nodded and rejoined my family.

"Beautiful," my aunt whispered. She tapped my hand. "Just lovely. You made Zeke proud."

After the service, my father and I escorted Zeke's wife to the front steps of the cathedral. She pressed one of Zeke's handkerchiefs to her eyes as the casket passed in front of us. It was hard to distinguish theater from what was authentic anymore. After today, I would take control of all the messaging. Today, she got her tears.

I turned when someone tapped my shoulder. "Knight, there's something you should see." It was Dante. A man who had worked for the family for at least a decade.

I gritted my teeth. "I'm in the receiving line."

My father had one ear in my direction. "Go," he ordered sharply.

"Yes, sir." There was no other option.

I stepped out of the line and followed Dante, slipping behind the church. "What is it?" My jaw clenched.

We rounded the corner into the parking lot. I spotted two of my father's men, arms folded, standing at the back of a Town Car.

Dante pointed and they popped the trunk. I stared inside. It reeked of urine and sweat. The man inside was bound, and his mouth gagged. He began to thrash when he saw me.

"Who is this?" I asked.

"He has information," Dante explained.

The sun beat down on us. It was the beginning of summer, but New Orleans didn't care. The heat was unrelenting.

"Then, I'd like to hear it. Let him talk." I motioned toward the gag.

He wrestled against the men's hands as he pulled the gag from between his teeth. "Water," he pleaded. His voice was strained.

I nodded, allowing the request.

They dribbled water over his lips. "Now what's the information?" I needed to return to the receiving line.

"He saw something."

I reached inside my jacket and checked my phone, as if this was mundane. Boring. I drew the sunglasses down my nose and tucked the phone back inside.

"What did you see?"

"It doesn't matter what I saw. They'll kill me," he pleaded. "If I say anything. I can't, I can't, I can't..."

I huffed. I looked at Dante. "I don't have time for this shit. Not at my Uncle Zeke's funeral. Get rid of him."

I said it casually. With cruel intention. I knew things would be different once my father's only brother had been killed. I didn't expect it to change me overnight. Despite the heat, it was as if ice had coated my spinal cord. I hid the instinct to shiver from the other men.

I turned to walk away. Dante's hand reached for the top of the trunk. The man screamed.

"I'll talk. I'll talk."

I took a long pause before turning around. "What do you know?" I asked patiently. This was his last and only chance before I walked away for good.

"I saw who shot Zeke."

I knew I wouldn't return for the wake. "Start talking."

CHAPTER 2
KENNEDY

I didn't like new places. I pressed the tortoise glasses against my nose to block the light. It was invasive and unwanted. I scooted lower in the bistro chair, slouching under a palm frond. The shade was hit or miss on the outdoor patio, but it was too crowded inside. I wanted space. Quiet. I wanted to wallow in the feeling of isolation.

"Thank you," I acknowledged the waitress softly when she delivered my espresso.

"Anything else?" she asked.

"No." I winced. My head hurt as I lifted it to take a sip. I was paying the price for the party I attended.

I didn't make good decisions in new places.

I dug through my designer bag for ibuprofen and swallowed a few tablets with the coffee. My phone chirped, but I didn't look at the screen. I couldn't. There were probably pictures. In fact, if I closed my eyes long enough and remembered exactly what I had done, I could see the cell phones freely snapping shots of me.

I didn't care then. I only somewhat cared now.

My phone chirped again. My eyes moved to the two men posted nearby. I couldn't go to a damn coffee shop without my father's detail. Their heads leaned closer together, and one of them whispered.

Shit.

The taller one walked toward me. "It's time to go," he announced. His hands clasped in front of him. I saw the blunt edge of his weapon when his jacket was pulled to the side.

"I haven't finished my coffee," I argued.

"It's your father," he replied. "You can bring the coffee with you."

"I'd rather drink it here." I didn't want to acknowledge my hangover to him, even though he had noticed it. It was his job to notice everything about me.

"That's not an option." His voice was flat without emotion.

The second suit had already walked inside the bistro for a to-go cup. He returned, dumped my espresso in it, and handed it to me.

I glanced to my right. The couple next to me stared. They must have been tourists. Surely, the locals were used to mob boss's daughters being dragged through the city against their wills. I didn't know New Orleans well. I didn't know how to read people here yet. No one in Philadelphia would have flinched.

I glared at the suits. "What is the emergency?"

"We can't discuss it. It's time to go." His answer was as vague and sterile as the first time he told me.

"So, it is an emergency?" I pressed. Only for a second, I let the possibility rattle around that my father might be not be feeling well. He had more and more episodes lately. He wouldn't tell me what the brown bottle of pills was that he kept in his breast pocket. I had stopped asking.

"I didn't say that. Let's go."

I had options. I could kick, scream, and make a scene in front of the tourists. Or I could leave with the suits, follow orders, obey and fulfill my duty. I hated myself for choosing the easier path.

The cardboard cup was warm. I clutched it and marched past the tall men, pretending I left because I was bored with the coffee shop.

"This way." He extended his palm to shift me toward the sidewalk.

"I remember where we parked," I hissed.

If he had been a family member, he would have spat back at me, but being on the payroll prevented him from stepping out of bounds. Instead, he held the door open to the backseat while the other suit started the ignition. I climbed in reluctantly, and he slammed the door. He tested the handle from the inside to make sure it was locked. Both men were new. I didn't even know their names.

The leather seat stuck to the back of my legs. I reached overhead to adjust the vent. I needed cool air. Lots of it. I caught glimpses of ferns drooping in the stagnant heat. The driver took one turn after another. He wasn't careful with the wheel. Maybe it was his way to teach me a subtle lesson. I was as lost as I had been when we left the house an hour ago. I didn't have a great sense of direction. It was another reason not to like new places. It was easy to feel confused.

My compass was off. The axis I relied on had been splintered and shredded. I stumbled through a new house, a new city, and a new life.

The black Escalade pulled up under the portico. I heard the water splash in the outdoor fountain as soon as the handle was unlocked, and I stepped onto the paver stones.

One of the new maids nodded as I strolled through the foyer. I thought I saw her curtsy. I'd say something about that another time. The house was built in the early 1900s. There were high ceilings and opulent hand-carved molding on the walls. It still contained the original pulley-system elevator and box of bells in the kitchen that was used to summon servants.

It was incredible that in less than a week my father and I occupied the house without a trace of a box or piece of brown wrapping paper. He liked these things. The lead-glass windows. The history of the house. The thick columns out front and the gardens on the grounds. The elevator was a talking point over cigars and brandy. The history of the house was a way to establish prominence. A foothold into New Orleans social circles.

I walked into my father's study, flanked by my bodyguards. He was on the phone. I wasn't sure he noticed I had entered until he held a finger up to warn me against speaking. I fiddled with my phone until he was finished.

His eyes landed on me. I refused to squirm in the seat. My father wasn't a large man, but he had the kind of gaze that was imposing. Threatening. Dark. His light brown eyes were as menacing as any set of black coal irises. He had a thin frame that he dressed in expensive Italian suits. I'd never seen my father's hair out of place, or a stain on his shirt.

It wasn't until the bodyguards exited that he broke the silence.

I slurped from the coffee cup.

"Kennedy." His finger tapped on the oversized desk.

"Yes?" My eyebrows rose. I realized my mistake when the headache pinched together at my temple. "You needed me for something? Are you okay? Are you feeling all right?"

"You know exactly why you're here."

I shrugged. "I don't want to guess."

His scowl had cut down men three times my size. Yet, I still pushed boundaries. I tested him. I looked for ways to press his buttons. I created these situations, and I hated them. Sometimes I thought I hated him. I hated my own father.

"We've been in New Orleans exactly one week, and you've already become cheap gossip."

I blinked. "I don't like those words. Cheap gossip? What does that even mean?"

His cheeks began to redden. "It means you have embarrassed me. You have no regard for who I am. Our family name." His palms flattened into the mahogany desktop. "There are pictures of you dancing on a pool table. Do you even play pool?"

I swallowed hard. "No."

"Then why were you on top of one?"

I couldn't stand the glare. I flinched for a second. But it was long enough that I lost the edge I had. I felt my stomach flip and my lungs strain for air. My palms became sweaty.

"You told me to socialize. I socialized." My defiance was cracking.

"You were drunk, weren't you?"

I used the manicured point of my thumbnail to carve my initials into the coffee cup.

"Answer me," he growled.

"Yes. I had too many glasses of champagne," I lied. I'd had shots of Fireball and some other hideous mix of liquor in a shot glass. "Okay? Is that all?" I began to rise to my feet. "I didn't even know anyone there."

"Sit," he muttered between clenched teeth. "They know who you are now."

"Dad, I'm not sixteen. This seems dramatic, even for you."

"No, you're not a teenager any longer. You're acting like a spoiled princess," he seethed. "Kennedy, we have uprooted the entire business. I am establishing myself in New Orleans. You are part of this venture. A crucial part. You can't get drunk and dance on pool tables. There are pictures of your night out. I have clients who could see you. What in the hell were you thinking?"

"Okay. So, this is about you."

"It's always about me." Our eyes met, and I knew I wouldn't be able to hold the posturing. My eyes stung, and my mouth went dry. "I hold the keys to your future. I am the one to pass on your fortune. I keep you safe. I am the head of this family. Damn it. You have no respect. None. And there is a consequence."

I jerked my head to the side. I didn't want to see when his fist pounded the table, knocking a teacup to the floor. My eyes closed and I held my breath. The china met the hardwoods and I heard the crack of fine porcelain.

"Kimble and Joseph will be assigned to you twenty-four seven."

"Who?"

His eyes narrowed. "Your new detail."

"Oh, right."

My father continued with the outline of my punishment. "The only social engagements you are allowed to attend are the ones I decide you attend."

I bit my lip.

"Your social media accounts will be stripped tonight. I've already called in IT to handle it."

"You can't do that," I protested. "I didn't post any of them on my pages."

"But you were tagged. You need to learn how to walk through this city like a ghost."

"A ghost or a prisoner?" I whispered.

My father rounded his desk and leaned over me. He had never struck me, but I always wondered how close he had been to slapping me across the face. Just one comment. One rude question. I was always within a breath of being on the receiving end of his open palm.

"You are the daughter of Lucien Martin. You will learn what that means. If I have to lock you in your room like a prisoner, I will do it. You are not a prisoner, *yet*."

The words made my skin break out with cool perspiration. I could feel it on the back of my neck and on my stomach. I didn't want him to know.

"Is that all?" I dared to ask a question.

"Tell Kimble you're going to your room for the rest of the day. You look tired."

I nodded as I squeezed between my father and the chair, but not before his fingers dug into the upper part of my arm.

"This is your only warning, Kennedy."

"I understand."

His fingers unwound, and I knew there would be indentations in my skin.

I tugged on the heavy door into the hallway. The maid was polishing a set of silver candlesticks.

"Mr. Martin dropped a cup," I informed her. "There's broken glass on the floor."

"Oh, yes. I'll get it." She tucked the polishing cloth in the front of her apron and walked briskly to the supply closet.

I absently turned to see one of the two suits only inches from me. "Which one are you? Kimble or Joseph?" I asked.

"Kimble," he answered.

"I'm going to my room to rest," I repeated the orders my father had given me.

He took a step on the massive winding staircase. "Are you going to watch me sleep? You're not really my type, Kimble. It could get awkward."

"I'll be outside your door." He pursed his lips together.

"And what about your sidekick?"

"He'll be here as well."

I huffed and continued up the staircase. "Seems like a lot of security for one person."

"You're not just anyone." We stopped outside my bedroom door. My father's personal attendant passed us in the hallway. Kimble's hand moved to the latch. "You're Lucien Martin's daughter."

I was reminded often who my father was. I groaned, slipped into my room, and locked Kimble out.

CHAPTER 3

KNIGHT

Assholes. All of them.

I watched them dance and drink through the windows. The house was lit up like a damn Christmas tree. My eyes moved from the top floor to the bottom. There wasn't a dark room in the old mansion. The street was lined with houses like this one. Wrought iron gates. Family crests hung over the entryway, meant to intimidate. Gas lamps flickering with false warmth.

"Knight, you going in?"

I turned when Parker Bastion appeared. I hadn't thought about who was on the guest list. I took another drag on the cigarette.

"I guess." I shrugged.

He stood next to me, trying to figure out what I was doing outside when the party was on the other side of the door.

"You kind of have to, don't you?" I felt my friend's eyes watching me instead of the house.

I blew a puff of smoke in the air. "Seraphina would notice if I didn't show for her engagement party."

"The in-laws have a nice place." He straightened the tie on his tuxedo.

I nodded. My sister was engaged to Brandon Castille. His family owned a steakhouse franchise that was well-established in the southern states. Brandon's mother's family was considered to be one of the founding families of New Orleans. My father approved of the match. I knew he had orchestrated it. My sister hadn't had much say in the arrangement.

"I hope Seraphina likes it. She's moving in here." I snuffed the cigarette under my shoe.

"That's rough." Parker slid his hands in his pockets. "Married at twenty-one and moving in with her husband's parents? Even if they do get their own floor, sounds like a shitty way to start a marriage."

I popped a piece of gum in my mouth. The mint immediately washed out the taste of tobacco.

"I need to get this over with."

Parker slapped me on the back. "They have free booze. It can't be that bad."

I chuckled. Free anything didn't have meaning to me. We climbed the front steps together. The marble gleamed. As the doors swung open, the music from the band blared. Parker and I had been friends since we were kids. We grew up in the organization. Each of us the first-born son, poised to take over one day. Our families were allies. Always a plus.

"Bar's this way. I'll be right back." I lost Parker when he disappeared in the crowd.

I strolled past the guests, looking for an easy exit. The

fewer the people, the better. That was impossible with this kind of setting.

"Knight, you made it!" Suddenly a blur of white hurdled toward me. It was Seraphina in a beaded gown. My younger sister wiggled past an older couple and threw herself at my chest.

"This is some party." I peeled her off me. Her blue eyes flickered. She looked terrified. The way she looked when I had once dared her to touch the drain in the deep end of the pool. She was only five then.

Seraphina tugged on my elbow, dragging me to an empty hallway.

"What's going on?" I asked. "Aren't you having a good time?"

"Are you still smoking?" She scrunched her petite nose. "I can smell it on you."

I groaned. "I'm not up for a lecture on cigarettes."

"It's gross. You should stop. And if Mother knew—"

I exhaled. "What do you need? Did someone drop a platter of hors d'oeuvres?"

"No," she snapped. "I don't care about the stupid food. It's this. It's Brandon and his parents. I don't know if I can go through with this." She picked at her nails. "It's too much. This family is crazy. I don't want to be a part of it."

"All families are crazy. You think ours is any better?" My hands landed on her shoulders. "What about Brandon? You two seem like a good fit."

Her long lashes fluttered until her eyes closed. I could tell she was trying not to cry.

"He's no different than his parents," she whispered. "Can't you help me? I don't want to marry him. Please, Knight. You have to do something. Get me out of this."

Seraphina didn't know about the fight I'd had with our father when he announced the engagement. He was part of the old regime. The old New Orleans that still believed in arranging marriages and brokering deals through offspring.

I sighed. "Sorry, kid. There's nothing I can do."

"But you'll be in charge soon," she urged. "You're next in line to run the family. Please."

I hated that she was begging for her freedom. I hated that she looked to me for salvation. I hated that there wasn't shit I could do about any of it. Soon was relative. My father was fit and healthy. He walked the golf course twice a week. He played tennis. Swam laps regularly. He wasn't even sixty. Uncle Zeke's murder still haunted us, even though it had been months ago, and his killers properly punished. Their families ruined and humiliated in the eyes of the founding families. It was considered justice. I still considered it a nightmare I couldn't escape.

I shook my head. "Try to make the most of it. You can spend Brandon's parent's steak fortune. That could be fun. Take your friends on a trip. Buy a new horse." She was an avid rider.

Her eyes welled with tears. "I don't want their fucking steak money."

"Seraphina, just hang in there." I didn't know what else to say. Should I tell her I had already threatened our father? That I pinned him to the desk in his office and hovered my fist inches from his nose? Did I tell her there was enough rage in my body to beat him until his nose fractured and his skull cracked? Was that the kind of thing that would help at her engagement party to a man she didn't love?

She leaned against the wall and quickly unsnapped a silver clutch. She began to retouch her red lipstick. "You'll get to marry who you want. You know that?" I heard the accusatory tone. The resentment. The anger my little sister had bottled up in her voice.

She dabbed the corners of her eyes to remove the smudged mascara before she snapped the clutch shut.

"We'll talk later. Your guests are waiting." I nudged her to re-enter the party. "It's going to work out."

She plastered a wide smile on her face. "Is this better?" She spun on her five-inch heels and stormed out of the hallway.

By the time I shook enough hands to make it to a spot on the terrace, Parker was on his second drink.

"What happened to you?" he asked.

"I got cornered a few times," I explained, taking the bourbon from him.

It was quieter outside. The bass from the band vibrated, but at least I could hear myself think. My eyes traveled the distance of the yard. The fence that bordered the property felt like a zoo enclosure. We were New Orleans's most exotic mafia families confined in one space. The Castilles had installed a pool, along with a cabana house.

I glanced over my shoulder. I saw my mother parting the crowd and headed for the terrace.

"I'll be back," I explained to Parker, as I hopped over the stone railing and strolled toward the cabana.

There were floating candles in the pool as well as some kind of exotic flower. I knew Seraphina hadn't chosen a single element of the party. It was all Mrs. Castille.

I shoved my hands in my pockets and kept walking. I made it to the pool house. I slung back the bourbon and left the glass on a table. I opened the door and closed it behind me.

I didn't expect the sudden scream when I stepped inside.

My hands rose in the air. "Hey, just another party guest. Didn't mean to scare you." There was probably a couple in here fucking. But as my eyes adjusted to the darkness, I realized there was only one person here.

One beautiful, alluring scared person.

"Sorry," she whispered. "I didn't think anyone else would come out here. It seemed deserted."

She stepped out from behind a stack of pool furniture. I almost staggered. I was caught off guard. She had the body of a goddess, dressed in a tight black cocktail dress. Curves. Long slender legs. Elegant features I swore I'd only witnessed in paintings.

"I'm Knight Corban." I extended my hand.

She smiled. "Kennedy Martin."

Her hand fit in mine like a glove. Soft. Warm. Tender. I wanted to thread my fingers through hers and pull her closer. Close enough to study her eyes. What color were they? It was too damn dark in here.

The door immediately flew open.

"Miss Martin?" A broad-shouldered man hurried next to Kennedy. His expression was serious as he discovered she was no longer alone. I dropped Kennedy's hand.

I realized he had brandished a gun, and it was only a few feet from my chest.

"What the hell are you doing with that?" I glared at him. "Put it down. This is a weapons-free event."

"Not for security," he argued.

"I see." I nodded. "Detail for Ms. Martin?"

Kennedy groaned. "Kimble, I'm fine. Put the gun away. *Now*."

The bodyguard was reluctant to return the weapon to its holster.

"I insist." I nodded at him. "I don't think the Castilles would be happy if gunshots ruined their party. They take offense to those kinds of rules being broken."

The bodyguard checked the safety, before tucking the gun under his jacket.

"Thank you." I waited for him to leave, but he remained next to us. "That's all." I pointed to the door.

Still nothing.

"You can go, Kimble. I'm fine. Just chatting with a new friend." Kennedy smiled. Now that the door was open and an outside light shone through, I thought I caught glimpses of emeralds in her eyes. Fuck. She was breathtaking. Light pink lips. High cheekbones. Her hair was swept off her shoulders and fasted in a rhinestone clip. It was honey blond with streaks of auburn.

Her bodyguard didn't want to leave her. It could have been the black dress she wore. No man would want to walk away from her.

"I'll be outside. Not far," he added. He ducked on his way out. He was a damn giant.

"Sorry about that. He's only following orders."

She didn't have to explain to me how it worked.

"Why are you out here by yourself?" I asked. "Not having a good time at the party?"

"It's a long story." She sighed.

I walked to the wet bar. "I like long stories." It was a hell of a lie. I barely had the patience to read texts. But if this girl had something to say, I wanted to hear it.

I rummaged through the liquor cabinet and revealed a bottle of vodka. "Drink?" I offered.

Kennedy nodded. "Yes, please."

I poured one for each of us and sat on the edge of the chaise, allowing room for her body to slide next to mine.

"Are you friends with the Castilles?" I asked. I'd never seen her before. I'd remember legs like hers. When she sat, the hem of the black dress rose along the tops of her thighs. I wondered if she was the kind of girl who ran miles with a personal trainer to have a body like that. Or was she naturally a knockout.

She shook her head. "No. Or yes? I'm not sure."

I chuckled. "What does that mean?"

She blushed, pressing the glass to her lips. Fuck. They were full and lush. "It means I moved to New Orleans a few weeks ago. I don't know anyone. I've met a few people, so I guess that's not entirely true, but not anyone here. My father isn't feeling well tonight, or he would have been here. I'm representing the family name. Those are the instructions he gave. 'Kennedy, you must represent the family name,'" she mimicked her father with a decent baritone voice.

"Ahh. A new family in the area? Interesting."

"Is it that unusual?"

"This is New Orleans. Everything is unusual."

She laughed. It was light and airy. For a second, it opened something in my chest. Her laughter pried apart something I thought was sealed with darkness.

"What about you? Bride or groom?" she questioned. "Which side brings you to the party?"

"Bride," I answered. "The bride's brother, actually."

"Then, I should ask you why you're in here and not at the party with your family. I have a good excuse. I'm hiding from strangers. You're hiding from everyone you know."

I could see Kimble's silhouette through the blinds. Every few seconds, he looked over his shoulder to stare through the window.

"Hiding? I don't hide." I took another swallow of vodka. I stared in her eyes. For a second, I thought I stumbled into an abyss. I didn't know where it could take me, and I didn't care. I wanted to keep falling and see where I landed.

"Will your sister be upset you're in here?"

"Yes," I admitted. "Very." If there was one person who needed me tonight, it was her. But I couldn't fight the wolves who surrounded her. She was lost to me. Lost to herself. Things would be different when I ran the family. But the original families couldn't handle a revolution now.

"You should probably go then." She licked her lips after another sip.

"Another minute." I leaned closer. I wanted to steal minutes. I'd take seconds if that's what I could grab. "Does Kimble go everywhere you go?" I asked.

She nodded. "Everywhere. Well, for the last two weeks he has. He's my keeper. An unwelcome addition to my days and nights."

"Did something happen?" I smelled her shampoo. I inhaled the lotion off her neck. The proximity made me drunker than mixing liquors.

"Not a security threat. It's my own fault. Just something stupid I did."

My eyebrows rose. "What was that?"

The way she looked at me made the world shift. I'd have believed there was a fucking earthquake if someone told me there was seismic activity in New Orleans.

"The worst sin of them all. I embarrassed my father."

Her gaze darted across the room. I saw the shadow too. I jumped back.

It wasn't Kimble barging in this time.

"Mother." I rose from the chaise. She held the train of her gown in her right hand. It draped over her wrist in cascades of rich designer fabric. It was likely she had paid thousands for the dress. It would end up in a heap at the back of her closet and never worn again.

"What are you doing out here?" She wasn't looking at me. However, she noticed Kennedy with a deep suspicious glare.

Kennedy stood quietly, taking the brunt of my mother's scowl.

"Having a drink. Welcoming a new resident to town." I grinned. "Have you met Lucien Martin's daughter?" I introduced my mother to Kennedy. "They've only been in the city a few weeks. We're getting to know each other."

"No. I haven't." Her chin jerked upward.

"Kennedy, this is my mother, Felicia Corban, the one and only queen of New Orleans." My mother had a love-hate relationship with the title.

"Nice to meet you, Mrs. Corban. Congratulations on your daughter's wedding."

There was tension. Pressure. They immediately disliked each other.

"We're about to toast your sister and Brandon. You're needed in the house. With your family. The Castilles have been asking about you."

"Of course." I extended my arm toward Kennedy. "Shall we? I don't want you to miss my father's toast. He's known for oratorical masterpieces." I winked and saw Kennedy

24

cover her mouth to hide her laughter. I was pleased she wasn't intimidated. The girl was impressive.

Kimble followed us across the lawn and into the party. His attention on us was as lethal as my mother's.

I didn't care. Suddenly, my night had gotten a lot more interesting.

CHAPTER 4
KENNEDY

W ho was Knight Corban? Why did I take his arm and let him lead me away from the only sanctuary I had found? The pool house was boring and empty. I couldn't make bad decisions and end up online as long as I kept a healthy distance from everyone. Why was I standing with his family during the bride's engagement toast?

I smiled lightly while clutching a glass of champagne. The vodka had already warmed my muscles. His hand rested on my hip casually. As if it belonged there. As if we had done this a hundred times. It was exciting. Thrilling. The way he navigated my body.

A member of the band tapped out a drumroll to gather the rest of the guests to the ballroom.

A few minutes later, a man in a tuxedo climbed the steps to the stage and took the microphone from the lead singer with a smile.

The audience began to clap. I heard someone whisper

behind me. "Raphael worked so hard on this deal. He looks happy."

"The Castilles offered him a lot for Seraphina. One of the highest bids I've ever heard. A marvelous trade."

Knight didn't flinch at the words. Although, I was certain he heard them as clearly as I did.

My stomach rolled. I wasn't naïve. I knew how family weddings worked. They weren't entered into over a candlelit dinner with a surprise proposal and a princess-cut diamond. They were crafted in the back rooms of hotels or cigar bars. They were broken down by family wealth and stock. By potential grandchildren. By property. By money. By greed.

Mr. Corban smiled at the guests. He lifted his champagne in the air. "First, Felicia and I want to thank Margaret and Louis. What a wonderful evening. Beautiful. Thank you for throwing such a wonderful party. Brandon is lucky to have you as parents. You have raised a son to be proud of. A man who will one day be the head of his own family with Seraphina by his side. Having a son is a blessing. An only son a gift from God. Cheers to Margaret and Louis Castille."

I thought Knight's fingers dug deeper into the fabric of my dress. I tried to pay attention to his father and not to him, but he was distracting. As distracting as any man I'd met had ever been. He'd walked into the pool house as if he lived there. As if everything around him was his to be used or enjoyed. The pieces were only coming together now. His father was Raphael Corban, the king of New Orleans. That meant Knight was the city's prince.

"To our beautiful Seraphina. Princess, you have made us so proud." I spotted Seraphina across the room from us on the other side of the stage. The awkward man next to her was Brandon. "Your mother and I are looking forward to your wedding day as anxiously as we waited for you to be born into this family. May you bless us with many grandchildren." Raphael grinned at his daughter. "And to Brandon, my soon-to-be son-in-law..."

The room echoed with jabs and jeers. I had to keep my smile in place. I hated this sexist bullshit. It happened at every engagement party. At every wedding reception.

He eyed the man. "You have been given a precious gift, my Seraphina. Be the man she deserves, and you will have a happy life together. You know how the saying goes. Happy wife. Happy life. Cheers." It was short. Sweet. A masked warning—don't fuck over my daughter.

"Cheers!" the crowd erupted, and the band started another song when Raphael tapped the band leader on the shoulder. A horn belted out the beginning of a slow jazz number.

Knight's hand flatted at my waist and drew me onto the dancefloor.

"We're dancing?" I gasped.

He smiled wickedly. "Looks like it."

"You didn't ask."

"Didn't think I had to." He winked.

He spun me until I was dizzy, and then suddenly my body was pressed to his, and I felt the burn of his palm against the small of my back. I was afraid to look in his eyes. Afraid that he might see how breathless I was after dancing for only two minutes.

Guys were always hotter in tuxes. That was just a fact. But when Knight first barged into the pool house, I would have thought he was equally as sexy if he had been dressed as the gardener. The lines of his jaw were sharp and definite. He seemed formidable. Self-assured. He had gorgeous eyes. I didn't think I could swoon over a stranger, but Knight Corban was a sexy specimen of beautiful masculinity.

His lips lowered to my ear. The blood rushed to my cheeks. My pulse raced.

"Think we could ditch Kimble?" he asked.

"Don't you need to stay a little longer?" I searched his eyes. Damn. Why were they so dark and deep? "Your mother seemed serious about the family obligations."

"She's serious about everything," he answered. Felicia Corban already scared the shit out of me.

"I don't want to cause any problems. Really." It was the first time I was allowed out since the pool table incident. It could be my last for a while if I screwed this up.

"I checked all the boxes tonight. I'm done with appearances."

I nodded. "If you're sure."

"Positive."

"Okay."

His eyes lingered on my lips before tilting my chin upward. I held my breath. "You are exactly what I was looking for tonight, Kennedy."

I smiled. "And what was that?"

"A way out."

I DIDN'T THINK it was possible to shake Kimble. Over the past two weeks I'd tried. I'd climbed out my bedroom window as if I was still a teenager. I found Joseph already waiting for me in the garden. I'd tried to blend in with a crowd of women in the ladies' room in a shopping boutique, but after thirty minutes, Kimble barged in and cleared everyone out.

I didn't fully believe it until I was sitting next to Knight in the front seat of his sports car, and there were no headlights in the rearview mirror. I continued to look behind us.

I exhaled.

"Better?" he asked.

I nodded. "You have no idea."

"I think I probably do."

"Oh, right. Must be hard being the royal family of New Orleans." Did he sense my playful sarcasm? I was terrible at hiding it.

"Are you mocking me?" I saw the sexy smirk on his face.

"Absolutely not," I giggled.

"Parker and I have ditched bodyguards since we were kids. It takes skill and practice."

"You say that as if I should be better at it." He didn't know how hard it was when there were no distractions. Kimble had laser focus on only one target—me.

He shrugged. "You're free. That's what matters."

I settled into the seat. "Free." I glanced at him. "Who is Parker?"

"An old friend. Shit. I didn't tell him I was leaving the party."

I smiled, satisfied I had identified the friend was a guy. "Should we call him?" I suggested.

"Hell no. He'll understand. We ran for a reason, and I know exactly where we can go to celebrate."

"Tell me there's lots of champagne, and I don't care."

He laughed. It was a rich beautiful laugh. It made my core quiver and my breasts tingle. Just who was this man?

"Are you even old enough to drink?"

"I'm twenty-one." My brow furrowed.

He nodded. "Barely old enough to do much."

I eyed him across the gear shift. "Is there going to be champagne or not?"

We stopped at a red light and I felt the heat of his stare burning my cheeks. "I will make sure there is the most expensive decadent champagne you have ever tasted, Kennedy." His grin was as sinful as it was inebriating.

I tugged on the hem of my dress. It seemed to creep up inches every time the car turned on a new street.

"Good. It's the one thing I like about New Orleans."

I thought I saw a look of shock on Knight's face. "One thing? You only like one thing? It looks like I have my work cut out for me tonight."

"I guess you do."

"I DIDN'T KNOW dive bars carried expensive champagne," I teased Knight from the corner of the restaurant.

"My favorites do," he answered. "Besides, it's a French bar, not a dive bar. Its owner would disagree with you. Ahh, here she is."

We had been met at the door by a woman who seemed close to ninety. Her hair was tied with a scarf that matched the one draped around her shoulders. There was only candlelight. I hadn't spotted a single lightbulb. A man played the piano quietly across the room.

"Thank you, Marguerite." Knight nodded at the hostess before she walked away.

"How did you find this place?" The walls were chipped,

and the paint peeled in long slow strips. The bar's countertop looked as if it was original, but I couldn't put a date on it. Maybe early 1800s. It was clear Knight loved this place.

"I know all the good places to hide." He winked.

"I don't see a name anywhere?" I looked for a logo.

"Marguerite's."

The champagne was sweet and crisp. It was perfect. The atmosphere was perfect.

"Maybe you can show me where they are. I need good hiding spots." The piano player stopped playing to light another candle. The wax splatters on the baby grand weren't appalling. They were charming. Almost eerie. He continued to play when the new flame jumped to life.

"I might be willing to do that. But on one condition." His voice dropped. It was almost too deep and low to hear. I leaned closer.

"You want to negotiate?" I pressed.

He nodded. "I want another dance. The first one was cut short. It was too crowded."

"Here?" I placed my champagne glass on the well-worn table. "No one else is dancing."

I watched as he rose from the table, his tall muscular body straightening. He shirked off the tuxedo jacket and carefully folded it over the back of his chair. I watched every movement. Every flex of muscle when he unclasped his cufflinks and rolled his sleeves above his forearms. God, he had tan gorgeous skin.

He extended his hand. "Come on. The beauty of it is there is no one to bump into. A dancefloor for two."

Knight's palm was wide and strong. He had solid fingers, beckoning to accept his proposal. My hand slid against his, and I felt the immediate tremor resonate between us. I stepped forward.

His arm circled my waist, and I swayed with the rhythm of his body. I didn't know if our movements were on beat with the piano. I didn't know if the few drinkers were watching. I didn't know dancing in a candlelit bar could change me. Dancing was supposed to be freeing. An expression. A release. Dancing with Knight was none of those things. With every step, I felt more connected to him. With every note from the piano, I felt an invisible thread tying me to him. As if the dance was a way to imprint the feel of his body onto mine. I could smell him. A mix of everything masculine, cologne, liquor and a trace of tobacco. I wanted to inhale every ounce of him.

As my lashes lifted, I thought he was posed to kiss me. My lips felt heavy and weighted from the way his eyes dragged over them.

The candle on our table flickered before a swirl of smoke circled. The hostess hurried over to light a new one. It was just enough of an interruption to create space between us. I needed space and air. I pushed off Knight to sit.

"More champagne?" I raised my glass.

He sat. His scowl was even sexy. He poured another glass for me.

"Where did you come from Kennedy Martin?" he asked, his elbows digging into the table. "What brings your family to New Orleans? Is it just you and your dad?"

I always struggled with questions regarding my family. My place in it. My father. It helped that Knight's family ran the same way mine did. When I tried to date guys in college, things always ended abruptly the second any guy suspected my father's line of work. It was too scary to date a mob boss' daughter.

"I finished my senior year early. My father wanted to explore expanding his business here. We moved from Philadelphia. It's only the two of us." I blinked. "That's my story. What's yours?"

Knight ran his index finger along my arm. It was a purposeful stroke as if he had chartered a course on my skin to explore. "I guess I'll answer short and sweet with short and sweet. Born and raised in New Orleans," he answered. "My family has been here for generations."

"College?"

He nodded. "Tulane. I graduated five years ago." I knew he was older than me. But twenty-eight seemed almost untouchable. It added another layer to him that seemed to push him farther away.

"Your parents..." I chose my words carefully. "They made sure your sister had a good match. A happy one." I bit my tongue. "Have they done that for you? Any prospective mergers?"

The darkness in his eyes was consuming. A depth of obsidian I'd never seen. I swallowed hard as if I had stepped into a pit knowingly and willingly. I was wading through it, with no tools to navigate this man's moods. Hours in, and I was in frightening territory, but I couldn't stop. I was drawn to him. I wanted to understand his reaction during the toast. I wanted to know what his father's words had meant to him. Was his life as twisted as mine?

"No. No mergers." There was bitterness in his tone. "I have privileges Seraphina doesn't. I plan to take advantage of them. Fully," he emphasized.

I didn't know why his answer made my heart beat

faster. It didn't help that he was sexy as hell. Tall. Cocky and confident. I didn't know whether Knight was as bad and ruthless as the players I always met in my father's world. Was he hardened and soulless? Did he spit out good people to make a deal? Would he spit me out when he was done? Was I willing to take that chance?

"It's getting late." My champagne glass was empty. Another round would be too much. I already felt light-headed at the engagement party.

"Giving up your freedom already?" he taunted.

The words clawed at me.

"I don't think you can offer my freedom. It was fun for one night. Thank you for introducing me to your hideout." I tried to smile, but the reality was suffocating. I was no different than Seraphina. Did he see it? Feel it? I wanted to own my destiny. I wanted to control my fate. My life. My love. I didn't have that kind of power; neither did his sister. But he did.

I looked away before my voice cracked.

"Kennedy?"

"Hmm?" My eyes drifted toward him again.

"I could drive you home, or I could take you one more place," he offered. "It's your decision, but I think we both know Kimble will be hell-bent on keeping an even closer eye on you after tonight. This might be your last night out for a while."

"It almost sounds as if you hope I'm locked in the tower." I peered at Knight.

"Hell, no. I just want you to consider that if you're going to go rogue, you might want to take full advantage of it."

My father was lying in his room, trying to recover from bronchitis. He was taking enough medication to sleep for a week. He didn't know I hadn't returned from the Castille-Corban engagement party. Kimble wouldn't want him to know he lost me.

I pinched my lips together. "Let me guess. You want to take me back to your place. Show me the spectacular view of New Orleans from your over the top penthouse."

He clicked his tongue. "No, not at all. But you paint a nice picture." His eyebrows waggled, and my cheeks turned crimson. "I could change the plan I had in mind. Yours sounds better."

Shit. He was intimidating. A smartass. A playboy.

"Let's stick to plan A."

He chuckled. "If you insist."

"Is it as quaint as this place?" I tested. I had already fallen in love with the French bar.

"Even better." He grinned.

"All right. If I'm going to face the firing squad over breakfast, I should at least have a good story to tell." I plucked my beaded clutch in my hand.

"Always my motto." His lips lowered close to my ear. "Carpe noctem."

I tilted my eyes toward him slightly. "Seize the night."

"What else?"

He guided me out of the bar with his hand pressed to my back. It seared as if he wanted to tattoo remnants of the night on my skin. But there weren't needles. Just protective brushes of his fingertips. I thought I knew exactly what motto he would have chosen to ink along my body.

CHAPTER 5
KNIGHT

The windows were down. I looked over as Kennedy lifted the clasp from her hair, loosening the twist and freeing the pins. Her tresses spilled over her shoulders in the wind. Fuck me.

I threw the car into another gear and pressed on the pedal.

It would have been a hell of a lot easier if her father wasn't part of the new blood moving into town. Kennedy was as defined by her role as I was by mine. I promised her a good time. I would deliver. We could deal with family ties and consequences in the morning.

I saw the confusion on her face when I pulled into the parking lot.

"What is this place?" she asked.

I laughed. "You'll see." We had driven farther out of town toward the riverbank. We were in bayou territory.

I walked around to the passenger side of the car and opened the door for her.

"Picnic tables?" Her head tilted.

"You've had New Orleans's finest champagne. Now you need to experience the finest oysters."

She shook her head as I led her to a table covered with a red and white vinyl cloth. "Oh, I don't know about that."

"Trust me."

She sat sideways in order to spin and thread her legs over the bench. A string of lights dangled over the table. I climbed in across from her.

I placed the remainder of the champagne bottle on the table from the bar. Marguerite had wrapped and bagged it for me on the way out the door. We waited for a server.

"It's after midnight. Why is this place still open?" she asked. "And packed." She looked left and right at the crowded tables.

"I told you. It's the best." I ordered a platter of oysters when the waiter arrived and asked for cups.

"You seem so normal," Kennedy commented. "It's weird how normal you are. It's almost scary."

"I am normal." I huffed. "Why wouldn't I be?"

She shook her head. "No. You're royalty. That makes you abnormal and hardly an impartial judge. I know what royalty means where I come from. In New Orleans, it's an entirely different level. So it's the French families in power here, not Italian. But the rules are the same."

I poured our champagne into paper cups. Kennedy's eyes widened when she saw the oysters on ice arrive.

"You eat this?" she pointed at them.

I winked. "You'll love them."

I could tell she was against the platter. She didn't like how they looked.

"Come here," I urged her to lean over the table. I topped an oyster with hot sauce and placed it on her tongue.

She cautiously closed her mouth. I waited for the reaction. The distrust turned to a smile.

"Okay."

"Okay?" I cocked my head.

"They're good." She nodded. "Really good."

I laughed. "My work here is done."

We drank and made our way around the shells on the platter. By the time we finished, we were the only ones still sitting at a table. The place was empty. The server cleared our table, taking the vinyl cover with him. I gave him an extra hundred to leave the lanterns on over our table and to close down the outside restaurant. I wanted to be alone with her. I couldn't give her total freedom, but I could give her a night of it.

"This version of New Orleans isn't bad." Kennedy dangled the paper cup between her delicate fingers. She was relaxed. At ease. She wasn't the same girl I had discovered in the pool house a few hours ago.

I climbed out of the table and strolled to her side. I sat, sliding my body next to hers.

I'd never wanted to kiss a woman as badly as I wanted to kiss her. Booze. Oysters. Starry sky. Crackling chemistry. Fuck. How did I show restraint?

"Knight?" she whispered. The question sounded like a command. I didn't like taking orders, but it was a plea.

I tilted her chin upward and took her lips with fierce ownership. My tongue lashed against hers. Kennedy dropped the paper cup of champagne on the grass and draped her hands around my neck. My mouth burned for her. I wanted to suck the alcohol from her lips. I wanted to drown in her. The purrs from her throat echoed in my ears. I nipped at her throat, inhaling her skin. Biting behind her ear and dragging my breath along her neck.

My hand traveled along her waist, following the lines of her curves. Trailing over her thighs. My fingers curled against her hip. My mind wandered as quickly as my hands. She tasted like champagne and summer. Innocence and purity in a world that was cast in darkness. Her body melded to mine.

"I want to take you back to my place," I growled against her neck. "Show you that over-the-top view I have."

She nodded eagerly. "Yes. I'd like to see it."

There was no guarantee she wouldn't be under lockdown for the next month. I had her in my hands now. I wouldn't waste what time we had before dawn broke.

It was another few minutes before we broke for air. I walked Kennedy to the car and kissed her quickly before shutting the door.

I tore out of the Cajun oyster joint and back toward the city. Neither one of us spoke a word. The sexual tension filled the car.

"This is it," I announced. I parked near the rear entrance to the courtyard. I lived alone, with the exception of a few members of my staff in a multi-level apartment. The ground floor was mainly for greeting guests or making them wait when I didn't want to take a meeting. My suite was on the top floor. And it did have a fucking incredible view.

Her eyes followed the windows to the top level. "As old as Marguerite's?"

"It's pretty damn old."

Kennedy was captivating. She intrigued me. And it had only been a few hours since she dropped into my orbit. I wanted nothing less than to take her upstairs to my bed, but it wasn't going to be enough.

I stroked the side of her jaw, craving her already. She blinked slowly before crossing over the console and wrapping her soft palms to my neck. My tongue thrust in her mouth, and we started drowning again. Her dress was bunched and dislodged around her waist.

The windows began to fog. My hands navigated her curves with recent memory. Her lips parted with a gentle sigh as soon as I slid between her legs. Finally, under that short little dress that had tortured the hell out of me.

She whimpered when my fingers made contact with the edges of silk. I strummed, working the fabric out of my way. Her hips tilted, and I had the access I wanted to her clit. Fuck, she was wet. Soaked.

Her eyes opened. Gorgeous green eyes, beckoning. Calling me. She stared, catching her breath. Gulping for air. But our lips crashed together, and my fingers went to work on her clit. Massaging, grinding, toying against the pulse of her body. My fingers swirled around her opening. Sweet, innocent Kennedy was going to be my undoing. I can't take much more of her moans without stripping the cocktail dress off her body. It was getting harder to maneuver in the car without climbing into the backseat. I doubted we would fit in the tight space. Breaking free from her seemed as impossible.

I dragged her lips from mine. "Let's go upstairs." I cupped her pussy, promising her there was more to come. "More room," I growled.

She nodded reluctantly. I wouldn't say the words out loud, but the energy between us was fucking insane. I didn't know what it was. I didn't know if it had a label or needed one. But the way she charged my body with kisses and long gazes. Whispers. Purrs. She was more than a one-night stand. More than a quick fuck. There was something about her I wanted. Hell, I didn't have to name it. No one was forcing that on me. Instinct was in control now.

I filled my air with lungs and unclipped the seatbelt. Kennedy wiggled her underwear and dress back into place.

I left the keys inside for my regular driver to park the car in the garage. I jogged in front of the hood to open the door and lead her inside my apartment. But I froze as soon as I heard the click-click of the gun.

I put my hands in the air before turning on my heels. Kimble was six feet from me. He had been waiting. I didn't know how long, but the fucker was ready for us as soon as I drove in. Had he watched us? Did the steam on the windows give us privacy?

Kennedy stepped out of the car slowly. "Put the gun down," she hissed. Her skin was flushed with sweat. I had kissed half her makeup away.

Kimble held the gun steady. "Not until you leave with me."

Her eyes darted to me. "I'm sorry. I have to go with him. I don't want to, but you understand?"

I reached for her hand. I wanted to pull her back toward me. To wrap her in my arms and hurl her inside my apartment. I would barricade the door. Kimble couldn't shoot his way through. No one could.

Our fingertips grazed quickly, but she was already at Kimble's side.

"Put it down. Now. I'm going with you." She stared up at her bodyguard. "You don't need to threaten him with a gun."

I saw the frustration welling her eyes. "You don't need to say anything to Mr. Martin about this, Kimble." I shoved my hands in my pockets. "She's safe. She was safe the entire night."

He didn't give any clues about whether he would take my suggestion.

"Get in the car," he barked at Kennedy.

Her eyes weren't the same. The openness was gone. The light extinguished. The wildfire we had lit had gone dark.

There wasn't a fucking thing I could do about it.

I watched as her bodyguard shuttled her into the Escalade and drove out of the alley. The tires screeched as he turned the corner.

Thunder clapped overhead, and lightning streaked across the sky. I didn't want to think about what almost happened. About how close we had come to setting our bodies on fire. The sheets. My bed. Fuck.

I turned for the back door and walked past Wallace, my house manager.

"Do you need anything, sir?" he asked. He had likely witnessed the scene.

I shook my head.

"I'm in for the night," was all I could manage to explain. I climbed the stairs for my suite and turned the handle. I glared at the empty bed.

THE NEXT MORNING, I beat my father to his office. He looked surprised to see me. I didn't work Saturdays. I kept to myself on the weekends, staying as far from my family as I could.

"What's this about?" He walked past me.

I sat on the arm of a leather chair.

"Do you have any idea how upset your mother is with you? You left before the photographer finished."

"Sorry about that."

"Are you?" His eyebrows arched.

"I was in plenty of photos. It wasn't even the wedding for Christ's sake."

"Try telling that to your mother. It was just as important to her."

I crossed my arms. "I'll make sure to check with the photographer before I leave the next party. How does that sound?"

"Who was the girl? Your mother isn't happy about that either."

I huffed. "What is she happy about?"

"She wanted you to dance with one of the Depas girls."

"Why?" My jaw clenched. "I've never been interested in them. You know that. Have you seen the Depas girls?"

My father shuffled papers on his desk. "Their father has recently increased his stock in a whiskey business. I think they're looking more attractive with those kinds of numbers behind their last name."

"Who cares?" I shook my head. "Not interested."

"You are twenty-eight years old." His eyes bore into my skull. "You can't keep this up much longer."

"Keep what up?" I drew a long breath.

"Dating. Running through girls like dirty laundry. You need to make an official declaration and start representing this family."

"I do represent the family."

He sat abruptly in the chair. "We have different interpretations of that word. You don't show the other families that you are committed. Where is the wife? Where are the kids? Huh?"

"Fuck, dad. I don't want kids right now." I ran my fingers through my hair.

He pointed at me. "You're almost thirty. I had two kids by the time I was your age. No kids means your legacy is up for grabs. You have no roots. No inheritance to pass on. You're going to end up like your Uncle Zeke. No heirs. No one to carry on your legacy. You're a man without legs if you don't have children. What are you doing to change that? What's your plan, Knight?"

I pinched the bridge of my nose with my fingers. "I didn't come here to talk to you about making you a grandpa. Okay?" My father had turned Zeke into a martyr, twisting and turning his tragic life to fit whatever scenario was in front of him. Today, it was that the man was childless.

"What then? It seems like the most pressing issue. I thought maybe after attending your baby sister's engagement party, it would have made you stop and think about your own future."

"It was a good party," I commented. "As long as Seraphina is happy, that's all that matters." Our eyes locked. He knew as well as I did that Seraphina was miserable. Neither of us would mention our last fight on the subject. It could lead to blows.

"She is happy," he snapped. It was a warning.

"What do you know about Lucien Martin?" I asked, changing the subject.

My father shrugged. His face was red. He had gotten worked up more quickly than usual.

"He's an outsider. Vulture type." I heard the contempt in his voice.

"Then why did you invite him to Seraphina's engagement party?" I thought the guest list was exclusively for friends of both families. Neither set of parents wanted to risk an event.

He pushed back to rock in the chair. "Because, always bring your enemies in close, son." I had been wrong about the guest list.

"Why in the hell is he an enemy? He just moved here."

"Lucien Martin has been buying up property for over a year. He might have just moved to New Orleans, but he's been trying to buy up the same sites we're after. He has five different LLCs, but Paul tracked them all back to the KM Corporation. He closed on his first hotel yesterday. He's driving up prices, starting bidding wars. He's becoming an issue."

KM? He had used his daughter's initials. "That's called competition. It doesn't make the man an enemy."

"It makes him a problem. A problem I need to dispose of before he buys up my next target. I was disappointed he didn't show last night. I wanted to have a word with him. I heard he sent his daughter instead."

Fuck.

My mother hadn't yet told him about Kennedy's identity. It was clear he had no idea who she was or anything about our meeting in the pool house. It was better that way for now.

"Why don't you let me take care of Lucien?" I offered. "Give this one to me. I'll look into him. See if there's anything from Chicago that might be of use."

My father eyed me. "You're offering to help?"

"Of course." I pretended it was a regular occurrence, ignoring I was usually reluctant to add more to my list of family duties.

"I'm glad to hear it." He sat for a minute, digesting the offer. "There's an auction next month. I want the property. It's a boutique hotel, but we need the access it provides. High-end clientele. Location. All of it."

"I know it." I nodded.

"Everything I've planned revolves around bringing the Vieux Carre into our portfolio immediately. We need the pipeline."

"I'll handle it. You'll get your pipeline." The organization had made millions. I didn't agree with trafficking more drugs under the city, but my father rarely turned away easy money. The Vieux Carre flooded and was reconstructed during prohibition. There were tunnels beneath the hotel that lead from the docks to the trucking warehouses. It was the perfect pathway for any future business operation he planned.

My father smiled. "I trust you will, son."

I left my father's office, not accomplishing what I wanted. Instead, I had a new problem on my hands. I had to hope that it would lead Kennedy back to me and not push her farther in her cell.

CHAPTER 6
KENNEDY

*S*omeone was blocking my sun. I peered over my sunglasses. It was Kimble. I couldn't tell if he was eyeing my new bikini. His shades were dark. His face expressionless.

"Yes?" I prompted. "What's wrong?" I stretched one leg along the other. My skin glistened in the sunlight. I hadn't had a say in the house my father choose, but I did like the pool. It felt as if I was in a French courtyard somewhere in the south of France on the coast.

"We need to talk about last night."

I sighed. "I knew you would tell my father." I picked up the book I was reading. "I'm not surprised."

"Actually, I haven't mentioned it."

I sat forward. He had my attention. "Why not?" I asked.

"Didn't you notice?"

"Notice what?"

"Your father hasn't left his rooms today."

I held my breath, expecting him to elaborate. "Okay. And your point?"

"It's almost one o'clock. He's not well. I don't want to add to his stress. I'm supposed to keep the Martins safe. I take that seriously."

I groaned. "It's just bronchitis. He gets it all the time." Of all the people to fuss over my father, I didn't expect it to be Kimble.

"Whether he does or not, I thought I'd give you a pass for last night. For his sake, at least."

"A pass?" I reached for my water bottle.

I saw the sweat trickle down his neck. He was wearing a suit, equipped with body armor and weapons.

"Yes. A pass. If he knew you had skirted my detail, we'd both be in trouble."

I laughed. "So, this is about you saving your job. It's not really because you're worried about his health."

"No." He shook his head. "I'm trying to do a favor for you too. He won't be happy if he knows you spent the evening with Knight Corban."

"That's crazy because he sent me to Seraphina Corban's engagement party," I argued. "He wanted me to represent him, and that means I have to socialize with everyone. Even Knight Corban." My argument was foolproof.

"You were there because of the Castilles, not to sneak off with Knight Corban."

How did Kimble know what my father's intentions were? "What are you talking about?"

"Trust me. Stay away from Knight Corban. I won't keep your secret next time."

I spun, placing my feet on the hot concrete. I rose slowly. I was certain I saw Kimble's eyes drag over my body.

"Why even tell me that?" I pressed.

"I probably shouldn't have."

But he did. "Thanks." I slinked past him, hauling my pool bag with me. "What's the other guy's name? The other one who is on my detail?"

"Joseph?"

"Yeah. Him. Does he know I got past you last night?" I was curious.

Kimble didn't answer.

I giggled. "I guess I'll keep that to myself then."

As I wandered through the house, I passed my father's room. The door was closed. I leaned in slightly, but it was quiet. I hesitated. I could knock, but something stopped me. I decided I'd check on him after my shower. I didn't need a lecture on my bikini. Or how I wasted precious time sitting by the pool.

When I turned, I spotted the oil portrait of my mother hanging across the hall from his door. He said he liked to see her every morning when he left for work and when he returned at the end of the day.

I stared at her expression. I wondered what was behind it. Was it love? Admiration? Resentment? I knew very little about her. Most of the stories I created about my mother's life revolved around this single portrait. It was the only display of her in the house.

What would she say now? Would she support my father? Those were questions I had asked a thousand times. Did she agree with how he used me? Did she think my value was tied to what family he could position me with? I walked away from her gaze, knowing I'd never have the answers.

～

It was another two days before I saw my father. He had turned me away every time I knocked on the door. This time, I took reinforcements.

Kimble used the key he had been given for emergencies and let me in my father's bedroom.

"Dad?" I tiptoed, then hurried next to him. He was hunched over, coughing.

He pushed my arm away. "How did you get in?"

Kimble was standing in the doorway. His hulking figure loomed behind us.

"We were worried. I haven't seen you. You aren't taking calls or meetings." The fact that it was the weekend didn't have any bearing on whether my father continued business as usual.

I glanced at the rows of pill bottles lined up on his nightstand. "What's all this?" I asked.

He shook his head. "It's for the cough. So, I sleep at night."

It was the first time I felt a buzz in the back of my head. An alarm bell. Something was wrong. It wasn't bronchitis. I nodded at Kimble to step out of the room.

"Dad, I think I need to get you in to see your doctor," I urged.

"No," he snapped. "Kennedy, I'm fine." He wobbled to his feet, and I moved out of his way. I didn't say a word when he grabbed the doorframe to the bathroom to steady himself.

"What are you doing? Where are you going?"

"I have a meeting. I'm going to get ready."

His silk striped pajamas looked like they had been worn for days. His cheeks were sallow. His voice scratchy and soft.

"I think you need to rest some more. Can't you reschedule the meeting?" I pleaded, surprised at the rising panic in my chest.

His knuckles turned white as he pivoted toward me without letting go of the arch. "Business continues whether I have a cold or not."

"It's not a cold," I argued. "You can barely stand."

He closed his eyes. But before he could fire back at me, I saw his knees buckle. I rushed toward him. "Dad!" I caught him before he slumped to the floor.

He groaned. It took all my strength to maneuver him back to the bed.

"Just leave me alone, Kennedy." He swatted at me when I pulled the comforter to his chest.

I placed my hands on my hips. "You need to cancel the meeting. I need to call a doctor for you."

His tired eyes lifted. "I can't cancel the meeting."

"You can't see anyone like this. They'll take one look at you and think you're on your deathbed."

Something in his eyes shifted, and I felt the zing again. What the hell was going on?

"You're still a child." Insulting me wasn't going to work.

"Far from it. What can I do to convince you to stay in bed, or at least call a doctor?" He didn't have the strength to make it to the shower. He would collapse before taking the first step on the staircase.

He grumbled and coughed again. I waited.

"You say you're not a child. Prove it." His voice was strained, but it was still sharp.

I folded my arms. "What does that mean? Anyone would take one look at you and tell you the same thing I'm telling you. You should not work today. Probably not for a while. You can call me names. I'm not wrong. You have to cancel the meeting. Reschedule it."

"This is why you're a child," he seethed. "You don't understand what's behind everything I do."

"Enlighten me."

"Our name is our legacy. I've tried to teach you that since you were born. We have our *name*. Sometimes that's all we have." He reached for a glass of water. "You take the meeting."

I blinked. "What?"

He nodded. "It's time you start training. I let you go to college. I've let you have a regular life. But our expansion in New Orleans needs complete focus. We could do this together, Kennedy."

I had never been privy to his business plans.

"What's the meeting about?" I dragged a chair across the floor to sit close to him.

"One of the well-established families has made an invitation. It would be suicide to reschedule."

"You're trying to impress them, or they are trying to impress you?"

He growled. "Are you able to take this seriously?"

"Yes, of course, I am. I'm just trying to understand all the angles."

"At least you've learned to size up the competition."

"If I take this meeting for you, will you promise to rest?" I asked. "Otherwise, I'm not doing it, and I'll call an ambulance if I have to." It was the first time I had threatened my father with something I could actually follow through on.

"No ambulance." His eyes hardened. "Yes, I'll stay here. You go. Take the meeting."

"We have a deal." I smiled softly. He closed his eyes

from exhaustion. Had he been suffering up here for days while I lounged at the pool and went boutique shopping? When did he acquire all the pill bottles? I thought about my conversation with Kimble a few days ago.

"Good." He nodded. "I'm going to tell you exactly what to say."

"You don't trust me to handle the meeting on my own?"

He glared at me. "I will give you the script."

"Fine," I relented. "Tell me what to say."

"Kimble will take you to and from the meeting. You stay exactly twenty minutes."

"Twenty minutes?" I questioned.

"Yes. It shows interest, but it also shows you are busy. Your time is valuable, Kennedy."

I nodded. "Okay, got it. In and out in twenty minutes." The meeting seemed more doable. The time limit took the edge off.

"Do not mention my health." It was a warning.

"I won't, but what do you want me to say when I show up instead of you? I think it will be obvious something is wrong."

I could tell he was thinking through the strategy. He wouldn't want to insult the family. He wouldn't want to be caught in a lie.

"Tell them I was called to Philadelphia for a family emergency that couldn't be helped."

I peered at him. "What was it?"

"What?"

"The emergency," I pressed.

He waved his hand in the air. "He won't ask."

I didn't believe him. People were curious. They always had questions and more questions on top of those.

"All right. What is the meeting about? What do we need to discuss?" I was concerned about this part.

"It's only an introduction. A family meeting. Have a drink. Tell him you love New Orleans. We're happy here and glad to be out of Philadelphia. Make my apologies for not being able to make it. That's all. Nothing more. Twenty minutes. And come straight here when it's over."

I nodded. "Okay. I think I can do that. What's his name?" I asked.

My father sighed. "Raphael Corban."

My stomach rose high into my chest. "Corban?"

"Yes. This meeting is important. Did you meet him at his daughter's engagement party?" His hand slid off the bed. I lifted it and placed it next to his waist. He was too weak to talk much longer.

"Not exactly, but I did see him." I thought about how to twist the truth.

But he started to drift in and out of sleep. I was glad the coughing had stopped.

"What time?" I whispered.

"Kimble has the details."

I stood from the chair and returned it next to the wall. I backed away from the bed, watching my father sleep. I didn't know how much time I had before my meeting with the king of New Orleans. The certainty I had that I could take the appointment evaporated when I realized it was Knight's father I would have drinks with, not a random boss in town.

I stepped out of the bedroom. Kimble was in the hallway.

"Do you have the meeting details for today?" I asked.

He looked at his watch. "I'll have the car ready to leave in an hour," he reported.

I took a deep inhale. "I'll get ready."

CHAPTER 7
KNIGHT

First rule of business: arrive five minutes early. My father had burned the lesson into my skull. Over the years, I realized he wasn't wrong about a few of his business principles. I found this particular one gave me an advantage. An automatic way to make the footing unsteady for my competitor.

I didn't know if it was possible to rattle Lucien Martin during this meeting. I also didn't have a clue what he already knew about me. What he had heard about my night out with his daughter. Did he know his bodyguard had wrenched her away from me at gunpoint? It was the reason I had stuck with last names when setting the meeting. There was a good chance he assumed he was going to have drinks with my father.

I didn't believe in chance. I didn't think for a second he hadn't blown into town without knowing who his biggest competitor would be—my father. It wasn't a coincidence they were interested in the same hotels, more specifically the boutique hotel.

I straightened the cuff on my sleeve. I didn't like the way it was pressed. I had to get Lucien to back off before my father used the full force of his business to shut him down. Under any circumstance, I didn't give a shit who my father decided to run into the ground. But this time I did. I wasn't interested in Kennedy being caught in the crosshairs of our fathers' business war.

I checked my watch. One minute.

I ordered a gin on the rocks and waited for Lucien. I dug in my pocket for a cigarette but then remembered the way Kennedy's nose turned up when she saw the pack. I opted to leave them where they were.

The bar I choose was old-school New Orleans. Heavy wood walls. Brass fixtures. A direct nod to the established families in the area. There was a side door that wafted with cigar smoke every time someone opened it.

The server delivered the gin drink on a tray and didn't say a word when he noticed the seat next to me was still vacant. Maybe business was done differently in Philadelphia. Lucien was nearly five minutes late. I shook the ice in the glass when the door opened.

The sunlight was a startling contrast to the inside of the bar. My chest tightened when I saw Kimble enter first. I assumed he was Lucien's top security aide. His head swiveled left then right. He nodded when he spotted me in the center of the dining room. He held the door open.

And then she walked in.

I rose to my feet, not taking my eyes off her.

She looked just as shocked as I was. She faltered in her high heels. My arm extended quickly to catch her. My fingertips grazed the smooth skin beneath her forearm. I lingered too long. Kimble cleared his throat. Shit. He needed to back off and let us fucking breathe.

She gave me a nervous smile. "I thought I was meeting with your father."

"I thought I was meeting *your* father," I answered. "Why don't you sit?" I offered her a seat.

Kennedy fidgeted with the cocktail napkin on the table.

"You need a drink," I stated. I ordered the waiter to the table. "You like champagne."

She smiled. "I don't think that's standard for a business meeting."

"There is nothing standard about this."

"I guess not."

"We both need a glass."

I ordered a bottle to be brought over quickly. I sensed her anxiety. It wasn't how I planned to see her again. Not like this. Not in place of our fathers. I'd never felt more like a pawn, even though I was the one who volunteered to play the game.

I waited until the champagne had been poured. Kimble stood near the entrance to the bar. I felt his eyes penetrating the space between Kennedy and me.

"How have you been?" I asked.

"Since the weekend?" Her eyes flickered.

I ignored her sarcasm. "Yes. After our evening ended abruptly. I'm sorry about that."

She returned the flute to the table. "It wasn't your fault. Since that night, there have been no more parties, and I haven't had a single oyster."

I chuckled. "That's terrible news."

"I did have a good time with you, Knight. But I don't see it happening again." Her cheeks turned a soft crimson. It was hard to keep my distance. I wanted to reach out and touch her hair. Stroke the side of her face. But I hadn't forgotten Kimble carried a gun, and his attention was directed to me.

"Yet, here we are." I grinned. "Together. Same table. Same bottle of champagne." I loved watching her lips curl into a smile. "What did happen when you got home?" I wanted to know what kind of consequences Lucien Martin doled out. It was a good sign that she was out in public.

She shook her head. "Actually, nothing. Kimble promised not to say anything about it. My father has no idea about our after party."

My head jerked toward the bodyguard. I was surprised. "What's Kimble's deal? Why would he keep that to himself?"

Kennedy eyed me. "He wanted to give me a pass."

I wasn't sure if that was true. "Interesting."

"My father said this was an important meeting. What did you want to discuss?" I noticed she continued to check the time on her phone.

"I think maybe I should wait and talk to him."

Her forehead crinkled. "Why? I'm here representing the business."

"I didn't think you had any interest in the family business." I shrugged.

"You don't think I'm capable?" she posed.

"No. I'd never say that." Whatever it was, it created a gleam in her eyes. A spark in a sea of emerald green.

"But all right. What does Lucien Martin plan to do with the Vieux Carre hotel?"

It was quick, but a noticeable squirm. She tugged on the edge of the red dress. "What do you want to know?"

"Why that hotel? What does he want to do with it?" The original blueprints for the hotel had been lost in a fire once prohibition ended. The secret of the underground passageway had been kept within a small circle of families. I wanted to know if Lucien had been tipped off.

Her lips twitched. "Why is that any of your concern?"

I leaned toward her. It was hard to be this close and not reach for her. I was impressed my restraint had lasted this long. The more minutes passed, the harder it was to not think of the way her lips tasted.

"What about the project by the docks?" I asked.

The corners of her mouth wiggled. "What do you want to know?"

"All of it." I waggled my eyebrows. "What does Lucien have planned for that area?"

Kennedy began to shred the corners of the cocktail napkin. She cleared her throat. "My father didn't send me to tell you everything about his plans. You must know that. I can't just lay it out there."

"But will you?" I asked. "What could I say to make you come around?"

She laughed, placing the empty champagne flute a few inches from her clutch. "To unlock all the secrets?"

"How about one or two?" I taunted.

She glanced at her phone. "This was nice. Thank you for the champagne, but I need to go."

I stared at her. "You can't be serious."

"Why not?"

"You just got here. We've had one drink. There's a good bottle of champagne to finish. Stay awhile. Or better, let's get dinner."

"Together?" Her voice squeaked.

"I think we can both agree we're not getting anywhere with this business meeting. Why not have dinner?"

Her eyes darted across the room to Kimble. "Because we both know what happened last time."

"Bring him with us." I nodded at the bodyguard.

"Really?"

"Yes. If he's going to be your security detail, then he goes where you go. I get it."

I saw her process the information. "And what do I tell my father about our meeting?" she asked.

"You could send him a message for me."

"What's that?"

"Tell him to back off the boutique hotel deal. It's not going to work."

Her eyes narrowed. "Why would I tell him that? He wants the hotel."

"But he can't have it." I tried to keep my voice clear and firm.

"What makes you think that?" she argued.

"He's new to New Orleans. I understand he doesn't know how intricate the hierarchy is. That will come with time. But my father wants that space. Lucien needs to let it go. He should step aside."

A bubble of determination surfaced on her face. "You're saying your father wants it, so he gets it."

I finished off the last sip in my glass. "Yes. That's usually how it works." My eyes settled on hers. I could tell she was offended. "Look." I brushed my thumb over her knuckles before she tried to pull away from me. "Our fathers' business isn't us. What they do isn't you and me. Our meeting is over. I just want to take you to dinner, Kennedy."

She exhaled. "You don't care that we're on opposite sides of this thing?"

"No. I don't give a shit, honestly. I'd like to take you out. That's all I care about right now."

Her bottom lip dragged under her teeth. "Where do you want to go?"

I paid the tab for the drinks. "You'll see. Let's get out of here."

CHAPTER 8
KENNEDY

I had chosen a red dress for the meeting. One that accentuated my waist and drifted up and down my leg at mid-thigh. I wanted Mr. Corban to know I was a force of nature. He needed to take me seriously. Red was a power statement. I wanted the dress to set a different tone than my gown from Seraphina's engagement party. I wasn't a party guest today. I was an extension of my father's arm. I was a part of the Martin dynasty.

I had to let the weight of that sink in.

I fidgeted in the backseat of the car while Kimble drove to the bar. I had looked in on my father before I left the house. He had already fallen asleep. I gave the house manager instructions to call me if he seemed any worse while I was gone.

Worrying about my father didn't come naturally. He made it difficult to care, much less show affection or concern about his well-being. It wasn't easy being his daughter. We didn't hug. He never tucked me in as a child. There were no sentimental father-daughter moments. But something shifted between us today. His eyes saw something in me they'd never seen before.

It was a lie to try to pretend this meeting didn't matter to me. I was nervous walking into the bar. Kimble's strong presence wasn't enough to calm me. I had to prove myself. I had to represent our family name.

The game changed in a single instant. The rehearsed pleasantries were useless as soon as I spotted Knight Corban. My stomach flipped, and I sighed quietly.

Did Knight have any idea how excited and anxious I was when I saw him sitting at the table instead of his father? I was relieved I didn't have to match wits with the king of New Orleans, but instead, I was faced with the danger of spending time with Knight. Not only drinks but dinner.

When I told Kimble to follow us in the SUV, I knew he wasn't happy about the decision. However, we were in town on my father's orders. I wasn't about to tell him the dinner had switched to pleasure, not business.

Knight whipped his sports car in and out of tiny side streets and alleys.

"Are you trying to shake my security again?" I asked.

"No." His eyes darted to the rearview mirror. "Should I?"

I smiled. Sitting next to him again, I remembered the thrill I experienced with him. There was something wild and untamed inside this man.

"I don't think it would be a smart way to start our business relationship."

He chuckled. "So that's what this is? Business?" I felt his eyes drift in my direction. "I thought we left that back at the bar."

"I don't know what it is," I answered honestly. It was quickly growing complicated.

"Maybe we should leave business out of it. It would simplify things."

"Maybe it would."

Once again, he drove me to a place I'd never seen or heard of. We were in the back alleys of the city. Before he had a chance to round the front of the car, Kimble was already at my door, scanning the street and keeping me in place.

"Relax," Knight instructed. "I know this place."

"Does this place know who she is?" Kimble eyed him. "I don't know that it's safe here. It's my job to keep her safe. I'm the one who protects her."

"As long as she's with me, you don't need to worry so much."

I pushed between the two of them. The testosterone battle was frustrating. "Just stop. I'm hungry." I stormed into the restaurant. Knight followed me.

"Why don't you send him home?" he suggested once we were seated. "He's a little obsessive about his job."

"I don't know that he'll listen." I held the menu under the candlelight to read it. "What about you? Don't you travel with bodyguards?"

"Yes."

"But, where are they?" I studied the guests in the dimly lit dining room.

"I sent them home after drinks."

"I never saw anyone at the bar," I argued. "Where were they? Who was it?"

He smiled. "That's how it should be. My team knows

how to fade into the background. They're virtually ghosts. Kimble sticks out. Everyone knows he's watching you."

I shifted in my chair. "He's following orders." I didn't know why I chose to defend him.

"But when does he start doing what you want him to do?"

"I'm working on it." I smiled wryly. I didn't like that my bodyguard was planted near the restaurant bar, watching everyone who walked in and out of the door. I didn't like that he was memorizing the moments of my dinner. I didn't like that he was witnessing how I interacted with Knight. It felt like a violation, not an act of protection.

A solo saxophone took a stage in the corner of the restaurant. I hadn't even realized it was there until the spotlight highlighted the musician. My breath caught in the back of my throat with the first note.

Knight reached underneath the table and stroked the top of my thigh with his thumb. I leaned toward him.

"I don't think I can do this," I whispered. I was suddenly filled with nerves.

"Why not? I think it's going well."

I lowered my eyes. "It's bigger than us, isn't it?"

I was afraid to look at him again. Afraid to feel my soul bounce around my body as if he had the other end of the string and tugged it when it suited him. It shouldn't be like this. Who gave up control this quickly?

"That depends."

"On?" I searched his eyes for something definitive. I didn't believe that there was anything but trouble ahead for us. The hotel was an obvious impasse. I was on a short leash, and as soon as my father found a family to partner with, I'd be married.

His fingertips trailed the side of my cheek. I pressed into his open palm.

"How much control we allow our fathers to have," he replied softly.

The saxophone hit a high note. I felt the shudder carry down my spine and to my ankles. "We aren't on equal ground. You have a say in your future. I'm no different than Seraphina. You realize that, don't you? I don't get to choose."

There was a hint of pain in his eyes. "What if we could change that?"

I held my breath, waiting for him to answer my prayers. I'd never accepted that I didn't get to choose my fate. I'd fought it since the day I discovered I was an asset to my father. A bartering tool. A dowry that he would pawn to cash in on a new business or set up a partnership.

I was fifteen when we attended my cousin Gigi's wedding. I was a bridesmaid. I was too old to be a flower girl. Too young to be responsible for any bride duties. It was an awkward age to be in the wedding party.

The girls took turns fluffing Gigi's dress in the foyer of the cathedral. It was a huge Catholic Philadelphia wedding. For a second, I held her bouquet. The flower girls had been ushered out. The photographer took pictures. Her father strolled toward her. I tried to hand the bouquet back, but Gigi was pleading with my uncle. She didn't want to marry Danny. He was nice enough, but she hated his big nose. He wasn't funny. He didn't like dogs. I tried to step away, but I was stuck with the bouquet. My uncle's cheeks turned red, and he raised his hand. I thought for a second he was going to slap Gigi, but he lowered it when she extended her hands for the flowers. It was as if he suddenly realized I was there.

I was as humiliated as she was. I whispered to her, but I didn't know what to say. So, I just told her she looked beautiful. It was all I could think of before I was tossed through the doors and expected to walk down the aisle ahead of her to organ music.

That night after the reception, I asked my father if he knew Gigi didn't want to marry Danny. I asked him if he knew Uncle Gio forced her into it. He loosened his tie and laughed.

"It was a good business deal for Gio. It doesn't matter what Gigi thinks of Danny. She's lucky," my father answered.

I didn't sleep that night. I tried not to think about my cousin on her way to Rome for her honeymoon, but she was all I could think about. I didn't want a Danny. I didn't want a honeymoon in Italy. I didn't want any of the things that were ahead of me.

I blinked. I didn't know what Knight thought he could control about my father. It wasn't possible. Didn't know Gigi's? Hadn't he seen this story end?

"Why don't we get out of here?" he asked.

"Another bar?" We hadn't even eaten yet.

He shook his head. "No. Something bigger than that."

"What do you have in mind? Let me guess. New Orleans's hottest dance club. Or a dueling piano bar, perhaps," I teased.

The way his finger traced my jaw made me shiver. "Far from it." The growl in his voice was nothing less than deadly serious. "I'm not talking about our date."

"I'm listening."

"It's summer. New Orleans is too damn hot. Let's get out of the city. Make our own plans."

"But we don't know each other." I studied his face. His gorgeous square jaw. His dark eyes.

"Worried we aren't compatible, Kennedy?" It sounded like a dare the way he said it.

I shook my head. The truth was I was terrified it was the complete opposite. I was scared he was the person that fit into my life in a way no one had come close.

"We can't take off," I stated.

His fingers wound tightly through mine. "We can. Pack a few bags. We hop on a plane and leave New Orleans behind. It's simple. We go together. Drink our way across Europe. Maybe spend time in the islands. We can go wherever you want first."

"Until Kimble finds me and drags me back by my hair." I dropped Knight's hand. "You know there's no way I can do anything like that. The consequences are too dangerous. Someone could get killed. My father won't stand for it."

He huffed. "Think about it. Think about what we could do this summer."

"I can't." I shook my head.

I wouldn't allow myself glimmers of light like that. It would only make the devastation worse when I had to succumb to the life my father chose for me. Some gangly man with bad breath. I'd started having panic attacks in the middle of the night, worried about who it was going to be. The move to a new city meant my father would be shopping around soon.

"It could be that freedom we talked about." He dangled it in front of me.

"This doesn't freak you out? The idea that we barely know each other and we're just going to hop on a plane to wherever."

"Well, you get to decide the wherever."

I scowled. "I'm being serious."

"So am I. It doesn't have to mean anything other than freedom, Kennedy."

"Everything okay?" Kimble appeared next to us. Shit. He scared me.

"Yes." I looked up at him.

"We're having dinner." Knight's jaw clenched.

"But it is getting late. I think I'm ready to go home. Our meeting is over. Thank you for the evening."

I caught Knight's expression. I would never be free. I would never be able to escape. The sooner he realized that the sooner he could move on. He needed to stop having hope.

Hope would only get us killed.

CHAPTER 9
KNIGHT

A week passed. Kennedy didn't answer her phone. Neither calls nor texts. She didn't respond to the flowers I sent to her house, or the bottle of champagne. I double-checked with the florist to make sure the address was correct.

I felt like a caged lion shut up in my apartment. I paced. I drank. On occasion, I sat in on meetings with my father. I listened to Seraphina complain about Brandon.

But nothing changed the fact that all I wanted was to see Kennedy. There had to be a way out. I searched the drawers in my apartment for a pack of cigarettes I'd hidden, but there were none. Fuck. I had given them up easily, but I couldn't give up her.

I grabbed the keys to my car and hopped behind the wheel. I drove until I was past the garden district. I never paid attention to these houses before, but as I grew closer to Lucien Martin's compound, I began to notice the old world stamp on the buildings. Classic architecture. Grand porticos and columns. Massive gardens and brick walls.

After a few minutes, I was buzzed in. The iron gate retracted, and I drove through the entryway, circling the front of the house. I knocked on the front door until a housekeeper opened the door.

"Yes?" She eyed me.

"I'm here to see Kennedy," I explained. "Is she home?"

"Miss Martin is out back in the courtyard. You can wait —" I didn't let the woman finish the sentence before I brushed past her and marched in the direction of the back of the house.

I slid open a glass door and spotted Kennedy lounging by the pool.

"And I thought you were busy." I stood next to her.

She slid her sunglasses down her nose. "How did you get in here?"

"Front door."

"No, I mean past Kimble and Joseph."

I sat on the lounge chair next to her. "I didn't see them. Why haven't you answered your phone?" I asked.

The beads of perspiration rolled between her breasts. Damn. She looked incredible in her bikini. She pushed forward in her seat.

"Because you want me to get on a plane to Bali. Or where was the last place? I think you said you had tickets for Amsterdam."

"You are listening to my messages. The tickets are just piling up."

"Of course I listened, but I can't go anywhere with you. Stop buying first-class tickets. That costs a fortune."

"I have a fortune," I retorted.

"I told you. This isn't going to work." There was defeat in her voice.

"You've given up before you even tried."

Her legs swung in my direction. My palms skimmed over her knees, planting her legs between mine. She tilted forward. I could smell the coconut on her skin. Smell the sun on her body.

She sighed. "If my father sees you..."

"Is he home?" I asked.

She nodded. "He's in his study working. I don't know who is with him today."

I brought my hands to either side of her face. "I keep thinking about your lips."

She smiled. "You do?"

I nodded, drawing her mouth close to mine. I pressed against the warmth of her mouth, soaked in sunlight. I parted her lips as my tongue twined along hers. Kennedy's hands wrapped around my neck, and I wanted to untie the string on her bikini. I wanted to worship her curvy body. Admire her breasts. Tease her pussy with kisses. I explored her body, gliding over it easily. The oil was a guide. My fingers curled to the inside of her thigh.

"Shh," I warned her.

Her eyes whipped open, but I tugged the bikini bottom out of my way and grazed her roughly with my thumb.

She bit her bottom lip. Her eyes locked on mine as I added another finger between her legs. I swirled her clit and eased inside her. She gasped when my fingers curled inside her.

"All summer," I growled. "Like this." I kissed her. "Free to do this." I nipped at her throat. My fingers taking on more territory. Her hips began to rock. I pushed deeper. The straps on her suit strained around my hand.

"I-I can't. Not here," she pleaded. Her breath was

ragged. Her eyes glazed over. "We're. In. The. Courtyard."
She panted hard.

I spotted a changing room, much like a beach tent in a
1920s movie across the pool.

"Come with me," I directed. As soon as I pulled my hand
away, she whimpered. But within seconds, I had draped the
heavy canvas curtain closed and tied the rope that held it
together. I pinned Kennedy to the wall with a kiss that
made my cock ache.

She clung to me as my hand reached inside her bikini.
She moaned when my fingers returned to that sweet spot.
Her tits jutted toward me as she arched against the wall. I
plunged into her pussy. My fingers were at work to make
her come hard in my hand.

"Be quiet." I bit her bottom earlobe. She squeezed my
fingers. Fuck. Her pussy was strong. Tight. I didn't expect to
be matched by her bursts of rhythm.

Her hair fell out of her bun and stuck to her shoulders.
She began to ride up and down. I watched as she tried to
take control of the sensations. The tiny whimpers she made
were driving me fucking insane.

"Shh," I tried to calm her and make her ignite at the
same time.

"Shit, Knight," she hissed when I flicked her clit like I
owned it. I worried we'd bring the cabana down with us.

I covered her mouth with mine at the first sign she was
about to come. I saw the shudder hit her. I felt the quiver
wrap around my fingers. I licked her lips. Kissed her. Held
her on her feet while she rode out the climax. Her eyes
opened with a long sweet sigh. I brought my fingertips to
my tongue.

"Fuck. I want to rip this suit off of you and kiss you. Suck you. Taste you, Kennedy."

"No," she whimpered. "Not here."

"I know. I know." I had barged into her father's house. I was dangerously close to getting a bullet in the back of my skull.

I pried her arms from me. "I made my point." I stood, trying to flatten out the rather solid erection in the front of my pants our situation had caused before I walked out of the changing room.

"You came here to make a point?" She still breathed heavily.

"I think I made it."

"And what is that exactly?" She stood, facing me with her hands on her hips. Hips that were tanned and slick with oil.

"That the only reason you're avoiding me has nothing to do with me and everything to do with what you're afraid of. We could do this. We could leave," I urged.

Her mouth opened in surprise. "How dare you."

I grinned, wiping the last bits of her lip balm from my mouth. It was watermelon flavored. "Face it. You're scared, Kennedy. What else would keep you here instead of out there with me?"

"It's not that simple." She yanked a coverup from the hook behind my head and wrapped it around her. She ducked under my arm and out into the sun.

"You aren't going to answer?" I followed.

I waited for a response when I heard the sharp footsteps behind. I turned to see a man not much taller than Kennedy with Kimble. Lucien Martin.

"Kennedy, what's going on here?"

"Dad, this is Knight Corban. He stopped by to say hello. That's all." I saw how quickly she walked past me to join her father as if there were an imaginary line, and she had to choose the appropriate side.

I hurried around the pool to extend my hand. "Mr. Corban, nice to meet you. I've heard a lot about you. Welcome to New Orleans."

The older man returned the handshake. "Thank you. Why don't you join me in my study?" He glared at his daughter.

"Actually, sir, I came to see Kennedy. Thought she might like a drive out to the beach. It's a good day for it. I'm sure you're an outdoorsy man."

He stared at my button-up shirt. "You're going to the beach like that?"

"I have a bag in the car," I lied.

"I think we should have that drink," he answered. "Kennedy, get dressed," he snapped. "Knight and I are going to catch up."

There was fire in her eyes, but I didn't know which one of us fueled it. Me, or her father. I wanted to pull her to me. To tell her I could still fix this. There was a way to sort through the family politics and find a way to grant her freedom. But those weren't words I could say in front of her warden.

I left her in the courtyard and followed her father inside the house.

He poured two glasses of bourbon and handed one to me. His study looked like my father's. Old. Dark. Classic décor.

"Thank you." I nodded.

He sat behind his desk. "I'm sorry I wasn't able to make

our meeting last week. Kennedy tells me you're interested in my boutique hotel acquisition. The Vieux Carre."

I wondered if she had told him everything we discussed. "Yes. That's true. The hotel is an important part of our development. I'm sure you understand."

I studied the man, trying to discern if any of Kennedy's features were in his face. Thank God I didn't detect a single one. She must look like her mother.

"I understand that Raphael isn't happy I want it. That's what I understand." He rocked slightly in the leather chair.

"New Orleans has options for you, sir. You aren't limited, but that particular piece of property. Well... you should know that if my father wants it, he's going to get it. There are lots of ways he can make that happen. You should back away before there's any bad blood between you two."

"Is that a threat?" His voice remained even.

"No, not at all. But since you're new, you might not realize how things work. In Philadelphia, it's possible you were the Raphael Corban of the city. If you wanted something, you could have it. That's not true here." I finished the bourbon and placed the empty glass on the corner of his desk. "The quicker you learn how my father runs the city, the quicker you'll be able to have a successful business here. Otherwise, you won't last. The original families respect him. They respect his wishes." I couldn't see where any of my words had affected him.

"But you didn't come here for me. You came because of Kennedy. You like my daughter?"

"Yes. I do. We've had a good time together."

"How old are you?" he asked.

"Twenty-eight."

"A little older than her. Are you sure you're not too old for her?"

"No. Definitely not too old, sir."

"Do you have any kids?" he pried.

I shook my head. "No, why?"

"I want that hotel." His eyes bore into mine.

"I'm trying to tell you as nicely as I can, that's not going to be possible." There were a lot of things that would go wrong very quickly for Lucien if he tried to hold on to a property my father wanted.

"You can have her."

"Excuse me?"

He pinched his lips together. "You like her. You can have Kennedy for the hotel. And I think we could make a few other arrangements to benefit both families."

I instantly broke out in a cold sweat. What the fuck? I didn't want to barter a marriage. I didn't come here to negotiate a trade. Hell, I'd charm him into letting me take her on a date, not spending a life together. I didn't wait for him to ask. I grabbed the decanter and poured myself a second drink. I refilled Lucien's in the process.

"What do you think? Tell your father I'd like to set it up. We can have a family dinner. I think that would be nice. I'll host. Let's say next week." He scribbled something on a piece of paper, but I couldn't focus.

I paced in the office, letting the bourbon burn my throat and make every thought I had fuzzier than the last. There had to be a way to work this. Barter freedom for Kennedy. Let her choose me, not be forced on me. This fucking hotel. The damn Vieux Carre.

"Here." He shoved the letter toward me. "Take it."

I'd never had nerves like this. The paper shook in my hand.

"I think you would be a good match for her. You'll take care of her. There's plenty of money. I saw how she looked at you. It's a good match. No need for Raphael and I to be rivals when we could be family."

I nodded absently without thinking about what I was answering. "I can't give this to my father."

"You will." He shoved his hands in my pockets.

"Why do you think that?" I folded the paper and placed it in the front of my jacket. My second bourbon was empty.

"If you don't, I'll tell Kennedy that you rejected her."

Mother fucker.

"You can't." I shook my head. I wanted a date. I wanted a night. Hell, I'd go as far as to say I wanted an entire summer full of nights with her. But what he was trying to do was more manipulative than my own father.

"I will. I'll tell her you tore up the offer to marry her." He leaned across the desk. "Want to test me?"

"She's just a girl," I whispered. It was true. A college graduate. Gorgeous. Smart. Sexy as sin. She had a decade to decide what to do with her life. It didn't have to happen here in her father's study.

"If you think she's just a girl, why do you call? Why send flowers? Take her to dinner? Show up like this?"

I rubbed the back of my head. "I didn't say she's ordinary. I enjoy her company. That doesn't mean I'm ready to look at rings. I think you're forgetting there are family rules at play. Rules you are eager to break. I have a say." I slammed my fist on the table. It was the bourbon surfacing. "I decide."

"You can decide. It can be Kennedy. Or not." He

shrugged. "I'll find someone else who will take her. Make no mistake about that."

I felt a lump, hard and painful lodge in my throat. The idea of Lucien contracting her to another family made me want to put my fist through the wall.

I glowered at him. "You're a bastard, Lucien."

"What happened to 'sir'? You're talking to your future father-in-law."

I only saw red after that. I couldn't stand the sight of him. I couldn't stand his voice. I charged out of the office and slammed into a maid in the hallway. Her dustpan clattered on the floor. I threw open the door.

I didn't expect to see Kennedy leaning against the sports car.

"Hi." She smiled. She had changed out of the bikini.

I moved past her, reaching for the door handle.

"Knight? What's wrong? What happened?"

I slammed it closed. "I can't talk."

"Wait." She pressed her hands against the driver's door. "Have you been drinking? What's wrong? My father said something. What? Just tell me. Or let me drive you home, and then you can tell me," she pleaded. "Don't go like this, Knight."

But I couldn't listen to her any more than I could to her father. I spun out of the circle drive and away from the Martin mansion.

CHAPTER 10
KENNEDY

"What did you say to Knight Corban?" I demanded an answer from my father. His gaze was out the window. He watched one of the gardeners trim rose bushes. The brown clippings fell around the man's boots. He stooped, collecting them in a bucket.

"It was an introduction. We got further than I expected." He hadn't turned to look at me.

"What does that mean?" I had changed into a sundress while he and Knight spoke.

"Don't worry about it. Everything will be fine."

"It doesn't feel fine." I was good at reading my father's moods, but I couldn't read his thoughts.

"I'm handling it."

I walked out of the office, not feeling reassured. I dialed Knight's number, praying he would answer. It went to voicemail.

"Damn it," I muttered. I searched the house until I

found Kimble and Joseph in the kitchen. "I need to go out," I announced.

"There's nothing on the schedule."

"I'm putting it on the schedule," I snapped. "Who wants to drive?"

Joseph looked at the other bodyguard. "I'll go," he volunteered, but Kimble intervened.

"No. I'll go."

"I don't care who drives me." I sighed. "But let's go. Now." I stormed past them, through the tiled mudroom, and into the garage. I climbed into the back of the closest SUV and waited for them to follow. I needed to find Knight.

I convinced Kimble to take me to Knight's apartment. I'd only been once and didn't make it any further than where he parked his car. I was beginning to learn that if I included Joseph and Kimble in my plans, they helped me. I wouldn't go so far as to call them co-conspirators, but they were at least willing to follow my orders.

I recognized the tall building when we pulled into the alleyway. Knight's car was parked diagonally in front. I hadn't been able to take in the features the first night. I barely had time now, but it was in a charming part of the city.

"Wait here," I instructed the bodyguards. "And before you say anything, you both know I'm not in any danger. I have my phone." I held it up so they could see it. "He has security. I'm perfectly safe." I saw the look on Kimble's face. "Do not walk into that apartment, do you understand?" I had to make it clear.

"Yes."

I exited the car and jogged up the stone steps. I knocked and was startled when a man with white hair opened the door.

"Hello."

"Hi." I smiled. "I'm here to see Knight. I'm a friend of his."

"I'm afraid he's not here."

I frowned. "He left his car out front. I just saw him fifteen minutes ago driving that car. He was at my house."

The man blushed when he realized he was caught in a lie. I couldn't blame him for covering for his boss.

I pushed past him. "Is he upstairs?" There were no noticeable doors in the foyer, only a staircase that led to the second story.

"Yes, but I wouldn't—"

I ran quickly to the second level. "Knight? Knight?" I stopped when I saw him sitting in front of a baby grand piano. The windows to the courtyard thrown open. Sheer curtains danced in and out of the room like ghosts.

"Knight, what happened?" I approached him cautiously. There was a full bottle of gin on the piano.

"I told you I can't talk about it." His back was to me. His broad shoulders stretched for most of the keyboard. I lightly placed my palm on his shoulder. He jumped.

"I just want to know what happened. That's all." I kept my voice quiet.

He shook his head. "No."

I took a step toward him, sitting on the edge of the bench so that my back was to the keys and I faced him. He didn't make room for me or acknowledge that I had broached his space. There was something dark and haunting in his eyes. It gave me chills.

"Please," I whispered. I didn't want to beg him. But nothing felt right. It was as if there was a fracture between us, but I didn't know where it was. How could I mend it if I didn't know how to find the break?

"No." He was firm.

"What about the tickets? The trips? Are they here? Do you want to show me?" I was trying to think of anything to shake his mood. To bring back the enthralling man I was falling for.

"I don't want to talk about the trip."

"What then?" I questioned.

His chin drifted toward me. I caught the hollowness in his eyes. A depth of pain I didn't expect to see. Not on him. Not on a man who dripped with confidence and charm. I didn't know any other way to erase it, but with my lips. I kissed him fully and passionately. I nipped at his mouth and lashed at his tongue with my own. Did kisses heal? Could this one?

I tugged on his shirt, quickly unfastening the buttons. I pushed it open, admiring the lines of his torso. The way muscle met muscle. Knight threw the shirt on the floor. I let my nails rake over his abs. He tossed my hands off his body.

I moaned when his fingers wrapped to my waist, drawing the thin sundress around my hips. My breath caught against his. My heart beat faster. The blood pumped in my veins as I crawled into his lap.

I felt the hard ridge of his cock through my satin underwear. I rocked against the bulge, closing my eyes. I wanted the friction. I craved it. I whimpered when he pressed my back into the keys and began to kiss my neck. His lips trailed my throat until he was between my breasts. The sundress fell to the side when he pushed the fabric out of the way. He palmed a generous portion of my breast.

"Ohh," I gasped as his tongue lapped before he sucked my tit into a hard point. He gazed at my nipples with lust, yanking the other one free and kissing it with roughness that made my body feel alive.

Our mouths met again, and he kissed me harder. With more force. More passion. It was as if there was something tangible swirling between us. A force of nature beyond our control.

The keys clanked as we moved together. I worked the top button on his pants, easing my hand inside.

"Fuck," he groaned as I slid my palm along his cock. If I could free it with some maneuvering. One thrust and he'd be inside me. Fucking me on the piano. I'd watch the pain in his eyes drain as the desire won him over.

"Knight," I pleaded as he pushed the satin fabric between my legs aside, circling my clit with certain strokes. He growled as he plunged his fingers inside me. I eased up and down, letting them fill me, stretch me. Things had ended too quickly in the cabana. I needed this. I needed him.

His teeth took my nipple with authority and I panted, knowing the more his fingers penetrated me, the closer I was to coming. I worked his cock, trying to concentrate on bringing our bodies together, but he was relentless. I lost control. I lost my senses. He yanked my hand from his pants and planted me higher on the baby grand.

"All I want is to fucking devour you," he growled. I should have taken it as a warning. I watched in awe as he peeled the panties over my knees and down my shins.

They tickled my ankles before he tossed them over his couch.

I slammed the keys with my palms when he spread my thighs. Our eyes met once before his head dipped, and he began devouring my pussy. The first swirl of his tongue was torture. I raised my hips, whimpering for more.

"Fuck me," he growled, diving between my legs again. He feasted. My knees wrapped around his head as his tongue darted in and out. My feet banged out notes high and low. A barrage of random sounds, louder than my moans.

I pressed into the baby grand. I needed leverage. Gravity. A way to belt out what this man was doing. He pried my velvet lips wide and ran his tongue around my clit.

"Holy shit," I hissed.

But he wasn't done. Every time he dragged his tongue over my clit, I thought it was it. Release was near. But he sucked. He nipped. I begged for more, grinding my hips toward his mouth. My nipples were hard and puckered. I dared run my fingers over my tits and I whispered his name toward the ceiling. My breath was ragged, and the juices flowing from my pussy were slick from him. From this unequivocally dominant sex god lapping at my pussy.

I was in heaven. Maybe it was hell. I couldn't tell the way my body rode the sensations. He kept me wanting. Needing. Pleading.

I felt the first quiver snap like the release on the end of a bow. I waited for the next vibration. My belly burned from wanting him so badly. Suddenly he thrust a thick finger inside me, and a long moan ripped from my throat. I'd never made that sound in my life. I couldn't hold off the orgasm any longer. I pounded the keys as it took over, crashing through me. Tearing at my veins. Breaking me. Ripping me apart. Knight pumped in and out, filling me, stretching me, kissing my clit and sucking my pussy until I was a ragged mess. A second orgasm tore through my body.

The keys clanked while his mouth made claim to me. My eyes opened when I realized my body had stilled. Knight was staring at me. He had lowered my legs.

I smiled at him. "Thank God. That was amazing." It had been building and building to this moment. Both of us climbing and clawing at each other with no interruptions.

"You should go," he whispered.

I shook my head. "I don't have to." The bodyguards would stay outside. He didn't have anything to worry about. I tried to reach for him. We had only just begun. I wanted all of him.

"Yes, you do," he corrected me.

He picked up the bottle of gin and took a drink. I watched him, trying to figure out what in the hell was going on.

"I'll stay. We can order dinner." I peeled myself off the piano carefully, making a loud noise against the keys anyway. I tucked my breasts inside my dress. They still felt raw and warm from his teeth.

"I can't. I can't do this. With you." His eyes cut to me, and I didn't understand. I'd felt the sting of rejection before, but not like this. Not after a moment like we just had. I saw the stiffness in the front of his pants. He hadn't recovered any more than I had. He wasn't done either. We were *not* done.

"Knight, just..."

"No," he barked. "You have to go."

He took another swig of gin. "How drunk are you?"

"Not drunk enough."

I tried to straighten my dress in place while biting the inside of my cheek. I didn't want him to see a tear. He wouldn't.

"Why?" I whispered. "Why even..." I couldn't say the words. I took a step toward the skinny French doors. They reached all the way to the tops of the twelve-foot ceiling. Knight's hand clasped around my wrist, stopping me from leaving.

"I didn't mean to hurt you."

I closed my eyes. "What was your plan?"

"To make sure you never come back." He released my arm and stumbled toward the piano. I watched in disbelief as he finished off the bottle and smashed it against the farthest wall. He started to play. It was haunting. As haunting as the demons I had seen in his eyes.

I didn't look for my green satin underwear. I ran out of the room and down the stairs. The door opened into the sunlight. Kimble and Joseph both waited outside the car.

"We're headed home." I ducked into the backseat. I refused to look up at the window as we drove away.

All I knew was that Knight had accomplished his plan. I would never come back.

CHAPTER II
KNIGHT

It was almost a week before I presented my father with the letter from Lucien Martin. I knew time was running out before he told Kennedy about the offer. I'd spent the week drunk. I'd spent it playing long ballads on my piano. I'd spent it sleeping off one hangover just to get to the next. I'd canceled meetings. Neglected work.

"What's this?" My father took the paper stained with drinks and food splotches. It hadn't left my hand.

I had showered and shaved before appearing at the office. At least I didn't look like a man who had been desperately lost.

"It's from Lucien Martin," I explained. "I told him it wasn't an acceptable offer." I waited for my father to read it. He folded it.

"He can't have my hotel."

"I know."

He shoved the letter in a drawer in his desk. "The Vieux Carre is critical."

"I told him you will have the hotel. I don't know what

else to say. He's not going to get it. There are lots of ways to make that happen."

"His daughter, though? Have you met her?"

It wasn't a question I expected. I nodded. "I have."

"And?"

"She's beautiful. Smart. Young." I looked at him. "Just graduated college."

"But you're not interested in a beautiful young girl?"

"The hotel is the cornerstone for your entire plan. Trading Lucien's daughter for that property isn't a good move for you." I couldn't even bear to say Kennedy's name out loud.

"What about for you?"

"I wouldn't do that."

He crossed his arms. "The bastard isn't going to have the hotel. I don't care if his daughter is a god damn Miss Universe playmate."

"I know, Dad. It's exactly what I said to him."

"Wait."

I paused at the door. I was ready for the meeting to be over.

"Last time Lucien came up, you said he sent an emissary in his place for the meeting."

"Yes." Fuck. He was putting pieces together.

"When did you see him then?"

"At his house." I couldn't lie.

"Some sort of follow up meeting?"

I shook my head. "No, I wasn't there to see Lucien."

"Why then?" he pressed.

"I was there to see his daughter."

He peered at me. "What the hell is going on, Knight? Your sister's wedding is in two weeks. Two fucking weeks.

91

I'm running around trying on tuxedos and eating cakes your mother puts on a plate for me. I don't need to worry about you getting fucked over by Lucien Martin's daughter. You have some thing for her after all? Is that what you're trying to tell me? Feelings? What is it? Are you just screwing her?" He shook his head. His face turned red. "The man is a con. He's not one of us. He never will be. He's about to learn the price for trying to interfere with my business. You don't need to be anywhere near that family."

I stared at him. "Five minutes ago, you wanted to know if I was interested in marrying her. Now you're saying she's off-limits?"

"His offer is rejected. No deal. No daughter-in-law." He pulled the letter from the desk and shredded it. I watched the tiny pieces float to the trashcan.

I needed space to breathe. "Okay, Dad." But it wasn't okay. And I still couldn't figure out why. "I'm out."

"We have dinner tonight with Seraphina and Brandon."

But I kept walking without acknowledging the family plans or the dinner. I didn't acknowledge his tirade. I didn't argue again about how he had decided on one extreme then the other. I had to find some air.

～

"I'm surprised you called."

"Sorry, man."

Parker shrugged. "It's been a few weeks."

"You know. Wedding shit for Seraphina." I had started lying to my friends. When had I become the asshole?

"I get it. I get it." He sat across from me. We had ordered pints at an Irish bar.

I wiped the sweat from my brow. It was hot as hell. The third day it had reached over a hundred degrees this week.

"Look, the reason I called is because I need some help."

I straightened in my seat. "What is it?"

Parker rubbed the handle on the glass as if there was a smudge he was worried about.

"Chelsea's pregnant."

I swallowed instead of spitting out the beer, and it lodged in my esophagus.

"Fuck, man, you okay?" Parker stared at me.

"Yeah. Yeah." I tried to inhale a full breath. "Sorry. She's pregnant? I didn't think you two were serious."

"We weren't." He hung his head. "But things happen."

"What are you going to do?" I was blindsided.

"Marry her." I saw the grin on his face.

"No shit." I couldn't believe it.

"Yeah. My dad is going to be pissed, but the grandchild is going to carry some weight being the first Bastion. Don't you think?"

"Yeah. Yeah. That will definitely help."

I stared at the bubbles in the beer. I was supposed to congratulate him. A baby. A marriage. We were the same age. We had gone to prep school together. College together. He was my best friend. He was headed down a path I didn't want a single foot on. I'd never felt more distant from him.

"You sure you're okay?" he asked.

"A lot of changes." I nodded. "Seraphina. Now you."

"It's not how we planned it, but she's having my baby. I can't walk away from that. And I do love her. It took a fight for me to figure it out."

"A fight? What do you mean?"

He shook his head. "I didn't react the way a man is

supposed to react when he finds out he's about to be a dad. Chelsea said she'd do this on her own. She was ready to breakup. It was then. Right then, when I thought I lost her, that I realized I was a fucking idiot. Who am I going to find better than her? You know?"

I didn't think that was the way marriages should be decided. Parker knew my philosophy on marriage. He witnessed the same kind of arranged bullshit I did. But bringing it up now would only be a punch to the gut. I kept my mouth shut. The truth was I didn't know Chelsea well. Maybe she was the perfect woman for him. They'd been sleeping together a few months. I didn't want to ask the obvious. Was he sure it was his baby?

The Bastions had money. Old money. New money. Loads of money. Parker was a target, just like the rest of us.

"I wish you the best, brother." I held my pint in the air. He grinned.

"Thanks. You'll be my best man, won't you?"

I didn't choke this time, but I wasn't ready for more commitment. "Fuck yeah. I'll be your best man."

We sat outside and drank another round. I left when I knew I could slide into the end of the Castilles's dinner party. I paid for the drinks as a congratulations gift and took off. Every stop I made me feel more lost. More distant. More remote from the people in my life. The distance was gaping. The trajectories of our lives had become divergent. And there was no fucking way to pull that back together.

CHAPTER 12
KENNEDY

" I want you to look at these." A folder fell into my lap. I glanced at my father. He was dressed casually today. It was Saturday. A polo and khakis made him look like he was outfitted for yard work. He rarely budged from his Italian suits.

"What?"

"Numbers on last quarter," he explained before walking away. "Go over them, and I'll see you in my office in an hour to discuss how we can project the fourth quarter. Take notes. Have them ready."

"Really?"

"Financials aren't something I joke about." His eyes were softer than his voice, but I knew to take him seriously.

"Of course not." I pressed my lips together. "I'll meet you in an hour."

I didn't argue, but I stared at the back of my father's head as he disappeared from the living room. I was watching a marathon of *Choose Cheer* before he interrupted. I pressed the mute button on the remote and flipped open the file. The spreadsheets were clipped together. I began to leaf through them.

I'd never seen his profit and loss statements before. Why now?

I sorted the reports into stacks. I only had an hour to make sense of them. That didn't leave me much time. I was also painfully aware I was still in my pajamas. My hair was pulled up in a messy bun. I hadn't bothered with makeup. I'd resorted to the same routine for days. A week actually. Since the horrible afternoon when I last saw Knight.

Something had to change. I couldn't continue like this. I drew the files into my arms and marched upstairs to my suite. I could apply makeup and read financials at the same time.

By the time I entered my father's office, Tammy, one of the maids, was on her way out. She had left a tray of tea. It was the full silver service, something my father usually reserved for important clients. Something that was hauled out and polished to demonstrate he had taste. He was as refined as any other man.

"Sit," my father spoke. He pointed to the table by the bay window. It jutted out into the garden close to one of the fountains.

"Over here?" I usually sat on one side of the desk, and he on the other. Always being scolded and instructed like a student.

"Yes, Tammy brought tea. She said you like orange. I've never tried it."

"I do. Thank you." I carried the file with me and sat at

the table. This felt off. I cautiously prepared my tea with a few cubes of sugar, stirring them gently in the fine porcelain cup.

The tea service had been a wedding gift from my grandparents. I'd heard about it several times. How much my mother loved it. How she liked to polish it herself, afraid one of the servants would scratch it.

I was always careful with it, but I could never bring myself to use my parents' wedding gift. It sat on the edge of the table. I noticed my father wore his readers. Glasses that he reserved for fine print and intense reading.

He looked over the frames. "All right. What do you have for me?"

"I didn't have much time to go into all the details in the reports, but I think I have a few things to share with you."

"I'm interested to hear what those things are. Specifics, Kennedy. I want to hear your specific thoughts."

"Right." I cleared my throat.

"Start with shipping," he directed. "You did read that report first, didn't you?"

One of the sheets of paper fluttered to the floor. "Oh, wait. I'm sorry." I heard him exhale while I crawled under the table, collecting my notes and pushed back into my seat.

"Are you prepared or not?"

"I am." I flattened out the sheet. My notes seemed frivolous now that I was about to read them to my father. "Okay, shipping." It sounded as if I was about to perform a book report in front of the class. Something I barely remembered, but the feeling was familiar. There was a knot in my stomach and the inescapable pressure to perform perfectly. On command.

My father's attention was sharp and focused. The words I chose mattered. Each one represented my analysis of the last quarter's shipping efforts since he had redistributed half the company to New Orleans. It was going to take another year to make the full shift, but that was part of my recommendation for the fourth quarter.

"I think it would be a good idea to keep a quarter of the shipping in the northeast. I know you intended to be a hundred percent invested here, but I think the last quarter shows that the northeast is still strong, and you can keep diversifying. It's safer and the profits are too dependable to shut that down and move it."

He folded his hands together in his lap. "What about the hotels? The boutique one. Vieux Carre. I'm sure you know by now the Corbans don't want me to buy it. They don't think I've paid my dues here."

I knew more about the boutique hotel now than I had when Knight first mentioned it.

"Dad, I think you should go for it." I smiled. "That hotel will symbolize your position in this city. You can't let the Corbans push you aside because you're new blood. There's nothing wrong with new blood. I think New Orleans could use a little bit of it."

His eyes widened. "Those are my thoughts exactly, but I was wondering what you would say." He grinned. It wasn't often I witnessed my father look genuinely happy. I saw his fingertips twitch as if he was considering reaching out to pat me in some way. Congratulate me for arriving at the conclusion he saw from the beginning. Only, he didn't know I was capable of sharing his business strategies.

I didn't either.

CHAPTER 13
KNIGHT

I surveyed the room. It was the usual collection of investors, along with a few new faces. The bank opened a second room to allow space for everyone to gather around two sets of oblong tables. I knew it would be crowded. I knew the auction would attract a high level of clients. But I also knew I had spent the last few weeks making sure the word was out that Raphael Corban was going to be the owner of the Vieux Carre. There shouldn't be any threats of real competition. This show of force was for the bank clients who didn't realize who they were up against. The bank expected us. I assumed we would be out of here in thirty minutes.

Then she walked in.

I spotted Kimble first. He was easily a head taller than everyone else. He cleared the area before Kennedy walked in with who I presumed was her father's attorney.

What was she doing here? I had made it clear Lucien didn't have a chance in hell of getting this hotel. He sent her? What kind of plan was this?

The powder blue dress made Kennedy look innocent. Almost angelic. Her hair was pulled back in a low bun. Her lips and cheeks were a light pink. Fuck. She looked beautiful. I knew she saw me sitting at the end of the table, but our eyes never made contact. Could I blame her?

I had tossed her out of my apartment after bringing her to the pinnacle of vulnerability. I still wasn't proud of what I did, but it had to be done. For her sake. It had tortured me every night since. She was the last thing I thought of when I fought sleep.

Lucien's attorney held a seat for her while she positioned herself at the table far from me. I couldn't see her face from the new angle. Kimble stood outside the room. She wasn't the only woman present, but there were only a few others. She stood out. She was young. Graceful. Fucking sexy. Every man getting ready for the auction noticed her. It was impossible not to. If it had been possible, I would have shuttled her into the hallway and tell her this wasn't a good idea. She shouldn't be here. Lucien shouldn't have sent her.

I had to pry my eyes off her when the bank's president stepped up to the podium.

"Good morning." He didn't bother to smile. He shuffled a tablet on the podium until the screen behind him was illuminated with the name of the bank and the property number. It was a stark contrast to the brightness of the room when the lights were turned off.

"You are here because of property 6-4-3-2-1-1."

I just wanted him to start the bidding. Get the charade over with. Paul sat next to me. He had instructions from my father to annihilate anyone who came close to the hotel. I was there to represent the Corban name. To demonstrate the family solidarity. Paul had been my father's legal counsel since I was a kid. A deal never floated across the desk that didn't have his eyes on it.

The president continued to list the features of the hotel along with the tax codes and the registration numbers for the auction. Formalities bored me. From the corner of my eye, I saw Kennedy scribbling notes as quickly as the president spoke. She didn't need to put herself through this. It was unnecessary.

I stared at the podium. The president opened the bidding. I sat back, letting Paul handle our first bid.

The Martin attorney made a motion. I leaned near Paul.

"Hold off until he's finished," I instructed.

Paul nodded. "You know him?"

"I know the family," I whispered.

"Anything I should know about them?" he asked.

"They're new. Shouldn't be a problem." But I underestimated Lucien's plans. I underestimated how he would react after I rejected his proposal. I rejected his daughter. He was out for blood today. He sent Kennedy in as the assassin.

I couldn't wrap my head around everything that happened before it was too late.

Paul kept bidding, but Kennedy didn't stop. I was certain there was a cap for Lucien. He should have given her details on when to stop. She kept raising the price. It surpassed market value twice over.

Fuck.

"What do you want me to do, sir?" Paul asked.

"Keep going."

We were the only two in the room left bidding on the hotel. She didn't know what she was doing. What consequences she was unleashing.

"It's too much," Paul whispered. "This is going to create a deficit I won't be able to fix for your father."

I growled. It was obvious she wasn't letting go of the hotel. I wondered if she knew about her father's offer to marry her off in exchange for the property. Did she have fuel of her own?

"We can't back down," I argued.

Paul shook his head. "I can't. They are going higher than anyone in their right mind."

I let my head fall. "Fine. Let it go."

I shoved back from the table and strolled out of the room. I left Paul to clean up the mess.

I waited outside the bank. I reached in my pocket for a cigarette. The smoke swirled into the air. I resisted the urge to punch the marble pillars marking the entrance. I didn't know if I waited too long on purpose or if I lost track of time. The doors opened, and Kennedy descended the steps.

"What did you do?" I confronted her.

I couldn't read her emotions with the sunglasses pulled over her eyes. Kimble flanked her side.

"I just bought a hotel." But I didn't see a smile or any sign of pleasure from her when she spoke the words.

"We should talk about this."

She turned away from me. "It's done. There's nothing to talk about. You made it clear the last time I saw you."

"Kennedy, no."

Kimble stepped in between us. His hulking frame was a pain in the ass. It was pointless to shove him out of the way.

"Drinks?" I asked. "Let's go talk. Alone," I urged. I threw the cigarette on the concrete step and extinguished it with my shoe.

"My father is expecting me."

"Let me at least apologize."

"For?" She brought the shades to the end of her nose. She motioned to Kimble to give us some space.

"You know what."

She shrugged. "I'm not going to do the work for you. If that's all you have to say..." She took another step toward the black SUV parked in front of the bank.

"No." My hand landed on her shoulder. "Forget the hotel. Just talk to me. Give me a chance to apologize for the last time I saw you. What I said. What I did. I owe you an apology." The guilt had chipped at my soul.

I thought I had her. I thought she'd listen. I thought the connection between us was strong enough to undo the fucking stupid mistake I had made. I was wrong.

Kennedy climbed into the back of the SUV. Kimble slid behind the wheel. The doors were locked, and she drove away without saying anything else. When I turned around, Paul was waiting at the curb.

"Ready, sir? We have to tell your father what just happened."

I shoved my hands in my pockets and followed the attorney to our car a few yards away.

"I'll break the news to him," I offered.

"I get paid to do this kind of thing. I'll do it."

I buckled my seatbelt. "But you aren't the reason we lost the hotel."

"I don't know that Mr. Corban will see it that way. How can you be sure?"

"Trust me. I'm the reason."

∿

I WASN'T afraid of my father. I'd seen how he wielded power my entire life. He taught me those skills. Trained me to take over the business. I couldn't fear what I know so intricately.

I'd seen him cut men to their knees with quiet words. I'd seen terror cover their faces when they realized Raphael Corban had them by the balls. He couldn't make me cower. I only hoped Paul could hold his own because he was going to need all the backbone and spine he could muster to tell my father we lost the Vieux Carre.

CHAPTER 14
KENNEDY

I flopped on my bed, kicking the high heels that matched my dress to the floor. I was supposed to feel triumphant. We had won. But all I felt was shaky and uncertain. That look on Knight's face on the steps outside the bank. It almost made me crumble. Almost.

There was something in the way he looked at me that had nothing to do with business and everything to do with regret. I could see it. The darkness. The endless spiral of guilt. The plea to make it right. I pulled a pillow under my face to block out the thoughts clouding my judgment.

He had gotten under my skin. He was in my head. I thought about his lips and his fingertips. I didn't forget the hurt. The humiliation. I hadn't forgotten how he cast me out of his apartment like a whore. I'd never forget that moment. Only, I couldn't figure out which draw was stronger—the need to feel his breath. To look in his eyes again. Or the feeling that I was nothing but useless baggage, weighing him down. An obstacle to kick out of the way. I struggled to weigh the emotions. I was drowning in them. Tumbling through the darkness Knight had laid at my feet.

I lifted my head when I heard the knock on my door. "Miss Martin?"

"Yes," I squeaked.

"Your father says dinner is at six."

"Okay." I couldn't stop the hard lump in the back of my throat from forming.

"He wants you to dress up. He's taking you out," Tammy reported.

My ears perked, and the pit in my stomach finally bottomed out. "What?"

"Dinner at six. In the city."

"Thank you," I called through the closed door.

I couldn't remember the last time my father and I had gone anywhere together in public. I knew he was pleased with the auction result. But this? It was a display of family pride I didn't expect. I scrambled off the bed and walked straight to my closet to pick out a dress. I had to put Knight Corban behind me. The Martins had made their mark on the city. It wasn't a day that would be forgotten anytime soon. By anyone.

"Dad, how did you find this place?" I asked over my menu.

He smiled. He rarely looked happy. "Did you think your father didn't know the good place in New Orleans?"

"Of course not." I grinned, but it faded when a tray of oysters was presented.

"Something wrong?" he asked.

I shook my head. "No. No. I like them. I just..." I didn't

want to admit that I'd had oysters once and it was a memorable night with Knight.

"Supposed to be the best in the city." He was delighted with himself. I didn't correct him. I knew where the best oysters were. And they weren't in a fancy restaurant. They were in a dive outside of town I'd never be able to find again.

"I'm sure they're wonderful." I held one of the shells in my hand.

"You know this dinner is a celebration." His eyebrows were high on his forehead.

"Oh?"

"You know this is about the hotel. I'm very proud of you, Kennedy."

My chest warmed. "It wasn't easy, but I'm glad you got the Vieux Carre, Dad."

He tucked the linen napkin at his collar. He had to wiggle his tie to make space. "There's something I think you should know about the arrangements. About how everything fell into place. Now that it's official. You should see the total picture."

We took a second to wait while the glasses of champagne were poured by our server.

"What do you mean? I thought the auction went well."

He smirked. "It wasn't that simple. I had to play a little game of chess ahead of time. It paid off." I knew how chess was played.

The bubbly happiness started to turn sour. "What did you do?"

He winked. "Kennedy, you know this move meant everything to me. Everything to the company. This is the home that you are going to create for the next generation of Martins."

"Well, that's not happening anytime soon." I hated when he talked about me like I was a piece of livestock to breed.

"This is where your dynasty begins. Your own legacy." He spoke as if we were in a hobbit book. Had the medication altered his personality? This was intense, even for him.

"Dad," I tried to quieten him.

He ignored me. "I couldn't risk losing the key piece. Not on the very first deal. Not when this one matters more than all the others."

My stomach flipped. I couldn't eat the oyster. I placed it on the bread plate. What in the hell was going on with him?

"Can you just tell me?" I asked. I'd never be able to guess.

My stomach plunged another level when I heard a saxophone start up. I searched the restaurant. The artist was outside on the street. The shutters had been thrown open. I wasn't the only one who noticed his playing. Small smiles lingered on the guests.

"Kennedy? You seem distracted. I'm trying to tell you something important. Something about your future."

"No, go ahead. You have my attention," I lied, tearing my head from the window and zeroing on my father. "I'd like to know about your game of chess."

"Good. Good. These are the life lessons that are the most important. Because I've made a decision. A big decision about your future."

"Which is?" I said a quick prayer that he hadn't met a premiere New Orleans bachelor.

He took his time making his way around the tray of

oysters. "See, I've realized something about you, Kennedy. If your mother were here, she would have said I told you so."

I blinked. He never mentioned my mother.

"You are a valuable asset to the company. In fact, you're going to be the face of the company."

"I don't think I understand."

It always bothered me the way he held his knife in his fist as if he used it to bludgeon someone rather than spread butter or cut a steak.

"You've picked up on the details and the reports quickly. You beat out every man in the city today for that hotel. And let's face it, I've had more bad days than good lately. I've had to start considering that."

He wouldn't say out loud what was going on with his health, but the reference was clear. I knew I couldn't ask questions about the pills that remained next to his nightstand.

"Dad—"

He raised his hand, still balling the knife in his fist. "Hear me out."

I nodded. "Okay, I'm listening."

"You might be able to secure a good merger to a good New Orleans family, but you're young. There's no reason to limit what you could do by setting up a marriage."

I knew my eyes bulged. I couldn't help it. "Really?"

"The Corbans played too many games. You are better than them anyway." He finished off his champagne.

"What? What does this have to do with the Corbans?" Specifically, I wanted to know about Knight. The restaurant seemed to darken. I could no longer here the sax player.

"I want the power in this town. I'm going to have it," he

stated. "My choices are take everything from Raphael Corban, or join forces with the bastard. I offered him a family merger."

My hands began to shake. "You made a formal offer? For me?"

"I did. But his son refused it." He seemed happy. Gleeful.

"When?" I gritted my teeth.

"He had up until the auction to make a decision."

I shook my head. "No. When did you make the offer?" I pressed for details. I had to force myself to accept what my father was telling me.

His stare was blank. "The day he stopped by the house. Our first meeting. We had drinks in the study, and I wrote the letter to Raphael."

Oh, God. That was the day. The day the light faded in Knight's eyes. The day he made me feel like the most beautiful enthralling woman before he yanked it away.

I pushed back from the table, reaching for my clutch. "Kennedy, what are you doing?" my father asked.

"I have something I need to do."

"Not the Corbans." He glared at me. "Don't go near them. Not now."

"Dad, Knight was important to me. Until you did this. I have to talk to him." I didn't feel like explaining where I was going or the million things going through my head right now.

"He made his decision. He doesn't want to marry you." The words hurt, but not the way he thought. I didn't want to get married right now, either.

I stopped along the side of the table. "These family rules are archaic."

"They have always been a part of our history. Our legacy. Your mother and I made a good match. Sit down. This is our celebration dinner. People are staring at you. At me," he hissed.

"I can't. I have to talk to Knight. You don't have any idea what you've done."

He scowled. "Sit down, now." I saw how his jaw flexed, and his eyes flickered with anger.

"But—"

"Sit."

I found myself taking small steps backward until I was in my seat once again. A wave of embarrassment heated my cheeks. I hated being scolded. Controlled.

"Stay away from him. Stay away from the Corbans. It's time you start your official training. My daughter isn't going to follow some playboy around town, making puppy eyes at him."

I had to bite my tongue at every insult.

I made it through dinner. I wasn't sure how I stomached the food. Everything tasted bland now that I knew what Knight had wrestled with for weeks. The champagne didn't help much either.

I had to bide my time until we returned to the house. Until the lights in my father's room went dark. I crept down the massive staircase and fired off a text to Knight. I didn't know if he would answer. But it was all I had. I couldn't risk showing up again, not after what happened last time.

I slipped out the patio door and ran into Joseph walking the perimeter of the property.

"What are you doing out so late?" he asked.

"Oh. Hi, Joseph." I was hoping I wouldn't find him or Kimble.

"Everything okay?"

"Actually, my dad needs some medicine. I'm going to pick it up for him. There's a pharmacy hat's twenty-four hours."

"I can do that for him. You don't need to go out."

"No," I snapped. "He's a very private man. You know that. He asked me to personally handle it. He doesn't want you snooping, Joseph."

If he hesitated another second, there was a chance I'd have to lie my way through this again. I didn't want either of my bodyguards with me tonight.

"Can I get the car ready for you?" he offered.

I smiled. "Yes, that would be great."

I thanked Joseph when he wheeled up to the front of the house with the car.

"Call if you need anything," he added, shutting the door behind me.

"I will. I won't be gone long." I put the car in drive and edge my way out of the driveway, making the turn more cautiously than usual.

There was still no response from Knight, but I had to believe he read my text, and he would meet me.

CHAPTER 15
KNIGHT

The last suitcase was in the back of the stretch car. My mother and Seraphina had pleaded one time too many for me to take extra clothes or snacks for the flight. I gave them each a hug and shook my father's hand. We had a formal goodbye family dinner at my parents' house.

"Call when you get to Paris," he instructed.

"I will."

Seraphina wrapped her arms around my waist and squeezed hard. I peeled her tiny body away. "I'll be here for the wedding." I kissed her on top of the head.

"You promise?"

"Of course. I wouldn't miss it. Not even for all the business deals in Paris." I saw my father's head nod to confirm I was allowed to come back. "It's the party of the century." She was scared. There wasn't anything to do now. Her future was with Brandon. She had to start to rely on him. She could have a partnership with him if she would only try. I wasn't going to be much help an ocean away from the family.

"We should get going, sir," the driver called across the car.

"But it's late," Seraphina argued. "Daddy, he could go in the morning." Her head whipped around to beg our father to change his mind. "Why take such a late flight?"

"No. The flight is booked. No changes." My father was immovable. He had been since he lost the Vieux Carre this morning.

I ducked into the back of the car. The cool leather was a relief. I stared straight ahead. I couldn't watch Seraphina cry. I didn't want to remember the agony on my mother's usually perfect face. I was surprised it was strained. Had she and my father fought?

"We'll be there in thirty minutes," Anthony announced.

"Fine." I looked down when my phone buzzed.

It was a text from Kennedy. I read it quickly.

"Anthony, I need you to stop on the way to the airport," I announced. The blood pounded between my ears.

"We're running tight on time."

I balled my fists in my lap. "I don't care. We're going to make a stop. I'll send the address to the car's GPS right now."

"Okay, sir. Are you sure?"

"Absolutely."

I linked the address to the car, and I saw it pop up on his screen. I reached into my carry-on. I had made one stop between the bank and my father's office this morning. The jeweler had called and said my order was ready for pickup. I tucked the velvet box in my pocket.

I didn't know what Kennedy had to say to me, but it better be worth missing the flight to Paris.

THE CAR STOPPED, and I climbed out. My legs stretched long. I heard the piano before I walked inside. Marguerite smiled. Her red shawl was pinned with a red rose tonight.

"Your lady friend is already waiting for you." She grinned knowingly. "I remembered her."

"You remember everyone, Marguerite." I stooped to kiss her on each cheek.

"I don't have that many customers," she replied.

"That's the charm of the place." I moved past her into the candlelit bar. My eyes landed on Kennedy, sitting at the same table we had shared nearly a month ago.

Her hair cascaded around her shoulders. It was blonder and more sun-kissed now than when we had met. She was wearing a black jumpsuit. She somehow made jersey material look sexy as hell. She was breathtaking in every way, and I had fucked up any chance we had.

"Hi." I stood at the edge of the table.

"Hi." She looked up. Her eyes shimmered. The flame on the candle sputtered as the wax dripped. "I didn't know if you would show up."

I pulled the chair away from the table. "I didn't think you wanted to see me," I replied.

I looked around. "Where's Kimble?"

"At home. I wanted to see you alone."

I sat. I wanted her to know how sorry I was we had traveled so far from where we started. I took responsibility for destroying the first glimmer of light in my life. For humili-

115

ating her. For pushing her away. For breaking her trust. I didn't know if I was strong enough to tell her all of it. It didn't help that Anthony was outside, keeping the car running.

"Thank you. For meeting me. I know it's strange after what happened today."

"What? This awkward? How you annihilated me at the bank?" I tried to smile, but there was tension in my chest, keeping my lungs from taking a full breath. It was hard to believe these were my last minutes in New Orleans.

"It wasn't supposed to be personal. It was business. Isn't that what you told me?" she asked plainly.

I shook my head. "It was stupid of me. Fuck, Kennedy. We became parts of the game. And neither one of us won today. We should have played it our own way. I'm sorry it's ending this way."

"What do you mean ending?" Her eyes darted back and forth. It was hard to imagine I wasn't going to see them again. The green flames I dreamed about.

"I'm taking the red-eye to Paris tonight."

Her face paled. "Why? For how long? When are you coming back?"

"I'm not."

"But that can't be—"

"It doesn't matter why. I'm leaving tonight and I'm not coming back to New Orleans. I'm taking over all the Corban operations in Paris. We have an extensive vineyard operation in the champagne business. You'd probably love it, actually. Did you order any? I can ask Marguerite to bring you a '98—"

"I don't care about champagne right now." Her voice tinged with rage. "You didn't mention Paris before."

116

"I didn't know," I admitted.

"It's because of the hotel?" Her eyes widened. "Is it a punishment? A penance? This is because I beat you today. This is about the Vieux Carre."

I didn't want to lie to her during our last meeting, but why make her feel worse? I shook my head. "I'm taking over the European arm. It needs to be done." I pressed my lips together. "But the text you sent. I thought I should stop by and say goodbye. Tell you I'm sorry about what happened at my apartment." The words came out mangled. If she had sent it thirty minutes later, I would have already been at the airport. We wouldn't be having this conversation.

"I hope you enjoy New Orleans, Kennedy."

"But you can't go. Not after what I found out," she whispered.

"And what did you find out?"

She exhaled. The candle wavered. "My father told me tonight about the merger offer. I know what he proposed." She scanned my face. "The offer." She couldn't say the words.

"Brokering our engagement?" I did the hard part for her.

"Yes. That. It's why you freaked out, isn't it? Still shitty, but what he did...what my father tried to do..." Her hands scrambled across the table, rubbing over the top of my knuckles.

She was making this harder than it had to be. I couldn't stop myself from tangling my fingers against hers. I leaned toward her over the table.

"Is that why? Tell me the truth. You threw me out of your apartment after the-the... piano because he tried to force you to marry me?"

117

I hung my head. "Shit."

"If you're leaving, can't you at least be honest?"

She had me. What did I have to lose? "Yes. I freaked out. For both our sakes. I knew it wasn't what you wanted or what I wanted. Not right now, at least. And to trade you for the hotel. I was pissed. I lashed out. I'm so sorry, Kennedy."

"Can't you stay a little longer?" she whispered. "We haven't figured this out."

"Figured what out?" I pressed my forehead to hers. I could smell her shampoo. The watermelon chapstick on her lips.

"What do we do now?"

"I get on the plane to Paris. You keep knocking 'em dead here, killer."

"That's it?" Her voice was too low for anyone else to hear.

"I'm sorry. I shouldn't have treated you the way I did. You deserve better. I owe you that." I felt her nails dig into my skin. She could tell I was trying to break away. I had to go.

"But I know why you did it now. I know why you lied to me. That changes things."

"Only part of that afternoon was a lie." I smoother her hair from her face. Our lips almost touching. "What I said at the end was the lie. What came before that..." My chest tightened. I'd dreamed about her body ever since I'd tasted it. "That was real."

"Then stay."

"I can't." Anthony would honk the horn any second. My lips burned for the softness of her mouth. Maybe it wasn't fair that I kissed her roughly. She was a magnetic pull that I hadn't been able to contest since the night we met at the pool house.

Her fingers feathered through my hair. She moaned. Our tongues tangled.

"Before I go." I reached into my pocket. "I had this made for you."

I handed her the velvet box. She cracked the lid and stared at the necklace. Her expression was both confused and excited. She held it close to the candle to read the inscription on the back of the pendant.

"It says *carpe noctem*."

I chuckled. "Seemed fitting after our first night." She fastened the pearl, encrusted with diamonds around her neck.

"And this is for the oysters?" she asked. Her voice cracked.

"Yes, so you don't forget the first."

"Knight..."

I kissed her cheek.

And then I stood up and walked out of the bar. I heard her call my name again, but I kept moving. Anthony was waiting outside for me.

"Sir, we're going to be cutting it close. You could miss your flight." He was leaning against the hood of the car.

"Just fucking drive," I ordered.

PART TWO

FIVE YEARS LATER

CHAPTER 16
KNIGHT

The lilies stunk. It was a putrid scent that wafted in and out of every room. There had to be fifty vases of the fucking flowers. The emerald wallpaper was dated, and the mauve carpet didn't help. I scowled at Paul. Was this the best he could do for my father? It looked like something out of a bad 80s movie. I was furious we were here. Furious it had been rushed. Furious at the damn florist.

My mother pressed an embroidered handkerchief to her nose. The netting on her black veil kept snagging on her wedding ring. "I still can't believe it. I'm so glad you're home, Knight. We couldn't get through this if you weren't here." She said it loud enough for everyone to hear.

She was a strong woman. She always had been. I wasn't sure I could trust that she was faltering now. But maybe death had affected her.

The first wave of guests entered the room, stopping in front of my mother before making their way down the line. Seraphina was at the end on the other side of Brandon. She refused to sit in a chair, no matter how many times Brandon tried to get one for her. It was still strange to see my sister six-months pregnant.

I hadn't had much time to talk to anyone, including her. I wanted to know how things were going with her husband. I wanted to know if our mother was putting up a charade or, was she actually crumbling? Who signed off on Paul's arrangements at this fucking funeral dive?

My flight from Paris landed with only enough time to drive to the funeral home before visitation began. I had changed suits in the men's room. I couldn't greet mourners wrinkled from airplane clothes.

Paul walked up behind me. "I've set up a meeting for you at the compound after tonight's event." His voice was quiet, so the other couldn't hear.

I nodded.

I knew it had to be done quickly. Raphael Corban no longer walked this earth. Someone had to make sure that everything he had built wasn't eviscerated in a matter of days. And that was exactly what would happen if we didn't act swiftly to transfer the power from his hand to mine.

"I will wait for you at the compound, sir."

He disappeared and left me to face a crowd of people I hadn't seen in years. Each one made up a kind story about my father. A funny tale. A classic Raphael memory. We shook hands. Some of the women hugged me and began to cry when they slid over to my mother.

I was relieved when I saw Parker Bastion. He slapped me on the back. "God, so sorry about your dad."

"Thanks. It's good to see you. Thanks for coming."

"I would have brought Chelsea, but she's home with

the kids, you know. We didn't think we should bring them to this."

"Right. Two kids. That's good. Good for you, man."

Parker rubbed the side of his face. "She won't care if I stay out tonight. It is a funeral, after all. Want to grab drinks? I'm buying." He smiled. "You still drink that bourbon, or have you moved on to French drinks?"

I didn't know if it was a quick kick of jetlag taking over, or if it was the foul smell of the lilies. I felt my stomach turn. I had to get out of this fucking line. I didn't want to small talk. I didn't want to pretend Raphael had one ounce of good in him. The lies invaded every corner of this room.

"Tomorrow night?" I asked, skirting away. "I have a meeting when I'm done here." I took a giant step away from the group. "We'll catch up then."

"Sure, sure," he answered, sounding confused.

My mother had already pulled Parker into a tight hug. I ducked out the side door and looked upward, trying to breathe in deep gulps of air. Thank God there was an escape out of that room. The humidity would take a while to adjust to again. This was nothing like Paris. I'd been home all of three hours, and I already missed the crisp air. Being in New Orleans wasn't supposed to get to me, but it did.

The door cracked. I heard the murmur of people talking. Coffee cups clanking on saucers. I didn't want to know who the footsteps belonged to and then I realized it was Seraphina. I smiled.

"Hey, what are you doing out here?" She wandered over.

I exhaled. "Getting some air." I draped an arm around her shoulder. "How are you doing?"

She shrugged. "Funerals suck. Daddy's seems to really

suck." Her hand rested on her belly. My little sister was about to be a mom. That made me an unprepared uncle.

"I can't imagine if he were here, he'd be happy about it. Where's the champagne? Cigars? Expensive scotch?"

She laughed. "It does seem really cheap, doesn't it?"

"I'm glad I'm not the one who planned it." Although he wasn't here to fire the staff. He wasn't here to yell and boil over until he broke fine crystal. He wasn't here to tell me I'd fucked it up.

"Paul was just trying to take care of things for Mom, but he's used to taking instructions from Daddy." Her eyes turned upward. "It's nice out here. Those people," she groaned.

"I know. How are you doing? Need a chair?" I teased.

She rolled her eyes. "Brandon won't let me ride. He told the stables to stop saddling for me. It's awful. You have no idea."

"I'm sorry. I'm sure the horses miss you too."

"Maybe you could go with me? I'll show you who I've added to the stables. I have an incredible stallion right now."

It was hard to tell her no when she was this excited. "Yeah. Let's go out there this week."

"Have you thought about what you're going to do?"

"About what exactly? There's a lot at stake right now."

"The will," she whispered it like it was a dirty word.

"Paul and I have a meeting tonight."

"What happens to Paris?" she asked.

"I don't know yet."

"Someone has to take over the vineyard operations."

"Since when did you care about our vineyards in France?"

I saw the way she pinched her lips together. There was something she wanted to say. Something she wanted to ask. I knew my sister better than anyone.

"What is it?" I prodded.

"It's just..." Her eyes darted to her belly. "Paris...if you need someone..."

The door to the funeral home flew open, and a man in a brown suit hurried toward us. I groaned.

"Mr. Corban?"

"Yes?"

"I need your signature on a few items," he explained.

"Our family attorney is handling everything."

"I can't find him."

Paul had left to prepare for our meeting. I looked at Seraphina. "We'll continue this later, okay?" I walked inside with the funeral manager. I stood in his dusty office for thirty minutes, signing approvals for the services already performed. I tossed the pen on the desk when I was finished.

"Thank you so much, Mr. Corban. I'm sorry I had to ask you at this time. I'm sure your grief is unbearable. Your father was a great man. A great man to everyone in the city."

I mumbled.

I left his office, ready to drive to the compound. The sooner Paul and I could begin extracting the paperwork for my father's estate, the sooner I'd be able to take control.

I walked past the receiving room. The staff was clearing out the coffee and the cake. Someone ran a vacuum over the faded oriental carpets.

"There you are." My mother's hand landed on my

sleeve. "I'm going to take my own car back to the house. I'm going to lie down."

I leaned to kiss her cheek. "Probably a good idea. Brandon and Seraphina are already gone?"

"Yes. He was concerned. He doesn't want her on her feet." My sister had never been fragile like crystal.

"I'll be up late with Paul. I'll see you at breakfast before the service."

She began to leave but spun on her heels. "We will ride to the church together as a family. You understand?"

"Yes." I slid my hands in my pockets.

"Good night, son."

"Good night."

The attendants continued to work around me. Once the vacuum stopped humming, I had to leave. I was the last one inside. I was struck by how quiet it was. Without the people crying. Without people scurrying to fetch coffee and more boxes of tissues. Somewhere in this building was my father's body. Cold. Lifeless. Alone.

The rain started slowly at first. One giant splatter followed by another. I watched it splash on the sidewalk. One. Two. Three. Throwing water. Making small wakes. I knew I couldn't observe time pass this way. The gutters began to fill, and the downpour began. I had to get to my meeting.

But the rain made my soul feel heavy. It made everything feel darker and more desperate. My life in Paris seemed so far away. Yet, the one in New Orleans was just as distant.

It kept falling harder. I pushed the door open, following the line of the sidewalk when I noticed where the sidewalk met the pavement.

One high heel stepped onto the curb. A slender ankle bound by a strappy lace that tied at mid-calf. My eyes traveled along her leg, dragging along toned muscle. Skin that I had memorized. Tasted. Touched. Her dress was swept to the side, gathered to keep the fabric from being soaked in puddles.

My eyes continued to roam, but I wondered if there was a way to make them stop. To stop myself from what I knew was at the end. To stop the inevitable. To stop the way the blood pounded in my veins.

"Kennedy," I muttered under my breath. She was somehow ethereal even in the darkness. Her movements airy. Graceful. Fuck. I had forgotten how she moved.

She held her dress in one hand. In the other an umbrella. Our eyes met. I saw the confusion spread across her face. Was it from me? Was it from the locked doors of the funeral home?

"Knight."

"Visitation is over," I explained. I didn't have words planned for when I saw her. But I sure as hell didn't think it would be those.

"Oh, my God. I'm so sorry. I should have been here earlier. I guess I got the time wrong." Her lips looked as edible as they always did. Lush. Pink. She let the umbrella tip sideways. It shielded half her face. I wanted to see her eyes again.

"It's okay. You didn't miss much." I wasn't sure how to answer.

"I'm so sorry about your father, Knight. I came to pay my respects to your family. I feel awful I'm late. I wanted to tell Felicia how truly sorry I am. My assistant sent a card earlier and flowers. Did my flowers arrive?"

It was then I noticed the dark shadow hovering behind her. Was that fucking Kimble? Five years later, and he was still lurking?

"Thanks for stopping by." The rain pelted my face. It was soaking into the collar on my shirt.

I was immobile as long as she stood in the rain.

Kimble took the umbrella from her and offered his arm to help her navigate the puddles on the pavement.

"I guess I'll see you tomorrow. Good night." She glanced at me over her shoulder while he escorted her to a black SUV.

CHAPTER 17
KENNEDY

"Everything all right?" Kimble asked as he steered out of the parking lot. The windshield wipers were on the highest setting.

"Yes, it's fine." I stared out the window but refused to look backward.

"You knew he'd be there." I felt Kimble's eyes watching me in the rearview mirror.

"I know." I folded my hands together. Rain had splotched part of my silk dress. "It was inevitable. It's his father's funeral."

"And yet, he still affected you."

I pinched my lips. "Nothing to worry about, Kimble. Just drive."

"It's just that he could be a problem."

I glared. "I can handle Knight."

"Does he—"

"Enough," I snapped. "Drive me home."

I tapped out a quick text to my assistant, Crew, to ensure the flowers I requested for the Corban family had been delivered. He responded with a confirmation from the florist. What did it matter? I slammed my phone into the seat.

Twenty minutes later, he pulled into the driveway, circling the fountain. It looked as if it was drowning in the deluge of rain. He continued into the garage. He turned off the ignition and walked around to help me out of the back of the tall vehicle. I watched the rain pour as he closed the garage door. It wasn't possible to shut out that kind of misery. I could still hear the rain.

"Ms. Martin, do you need anything?" Bella greeted me when I walked inside. She had only been on my staff six months, but she needed little training. It was an easy hire. "I could bring tea or a glass of wine?" she suggested. She looked concerned about the state of my dress.

"Yes, both." I smiled. "I'm going to change, but you can take it to my office."

After a quick curtsy, she hurried to the kitchen. I climbed the stairs, gripping the handrail. The top landing seemed as it was five stories up. *Knight Corban*. I closed my eyes. Damn it. His return had ramifications for everyone. I didn't know how to sort them yet.

The news of Raphael's death traveled quickly through New Orleans. Like everyone else, I assumed it would take a bullet to the back of his head for the man to die. It was possible one wouldn't have been enough. But a heart attack? It was a cruel fate for a man who had spent his life trying to guard against outside enemies. The irony was suffocating.

Our last meeting had been a month ago. He wasn't happy with me. He never had been.

I sat in front of my vanity and flipped open the lid on a

heavy marble jewelry box my father had given me when I turned sixteen. The stone was cold against my fingertips. There were hidden compartments inside. He had been pleased that it was intricate and unique. I lifted the velvet shelf from inside the box. I tapped a secret button. A door popped open. Beneath it was the pearl necklace Knight gave me the night he left.

I held it up to the light. The diamonds glimmered. I didn't remember exactly when I stopped wearing it. It had become a piece so dear to me I slept with it until I realized the engraving started to wear. Then I would take it off at night and place it on the nightstand. One day I woke up and didn't put it on. I returned it to the hidden square and closed the box.

I changed and slipped back downstairs, sitting in a chair by the fireplace. It was too warm to light the logs. I had made minor adjustments to the décor since I inherited the house. One was this oversized white chair. I could curl my feet under me and read reports. Sift through numbers and financial statements late at night.

Bella entered the room quietly and placed the tray carrying a cup of tea and a glass of wine on the footstool closest to me.

"Is there anything else I can do for you?"

"No. This is plenty. Thank you."

As soon as she closed the door, I reached for the wine. I scrolled through pictures on my tablet. My mind wandered, even when I tried to bring it back to focus. I had to change my schedule to accommodate Raphael's funeral service tomorrow. I messaged Crew to make sure everything was set.

I couldn't make the same mistake I did tonight. At least

I didn't stay longer than twenty minutes. I sighed, tapping my nails on the wine glass. The color on the tips matched the pinot noir.

Knight was going to be a major problem. But I'd give him the next forty-eight hours to grieve the loss of his father and finish the funeral services before he discovered what happened in the five years he had been gone. I could grant him that grace. It was the least I could do.

I DIDN'T WANT to sit close to anyone during the service. My presence caused enough of a stir. The Corbans didn't need unnecessary commotion. Kimble performed a sweep of the church, just like every organizations' security teams did before the procession began. He was satisfied with my seat.

I read the program, waiting for the priest to begin. The black gloves I wore made the pages rustle when I turned them. According to the inscription on the back, Raphael didn't want the traditional funeral parade after the church service concluded. It was true, it didn't suit him. But I was surprised the family wouldn't carry on with what the original New Orleans families considered their lifeblood—tradition. Original families claimed they were steeped in roots so deep no one could compete with them inside the city.

The wooden benches creaked as more parishioners gathered. I nodded at Seton Hiram and his wife, Priscilla. We had recently negotiated a shipping contract. I was impressed with his operations.

Camille Longrie hobbled in, tapping the marble floor with her cane. She smiled at me before taking the pew a few rows ahead of mine. Her husband was home. I was sure of it. Gerald Longrie hated Raphael. Sending his wife was the weakest attempt he could make to pay his respects to Felicia.

I cataloged the people as they filed through the open church doors. I had secured profitable deals with almost everyone in attendance. The few faces I didn't recognize I assumed were people within Raphael's organization that were on the bottom rungs of the ladder. I spotted his attorney, Paul, speaking to the priest. The mass should start soon. The family began to gather at the back of the church.

I quickly looked away when I saw the fitted black suit come into view. Shit. The jacket covered athletic toned muscle. It couldn't be disguised beneath mourning attire. He was still gorgeous and sexy. Finding him in the rain last night had cemented every memory I had of him. The sharp angle of his jaw. The darkness in his eyes. I hadn't forgotten how warm his skin had been when I touched it. I never forgot the way my body was drawn to his. I reached in my clutch for a peppermint. My mouth had gone dry.

Suddenly, the organ music surged from the balcony behind our heads. Everyone rose to their feet, and I became a participant in the funeral mass of Raphael Corban, my greatest adversary.

THERE WAS a great hall attached to the cathedral where wedding receptions were held, celebrations for baptisms, and funeral luncheons. I always thought it was odd that the funerals were lumped into the same category. They should have their own dark room with chippy tables and hand-me-down church linens. They shouldn't be allowed to dampen the happier life events.

I stepped into the hall, searching for Felicia Corban. Once my condolences to her were extended, I could exit quickly and make the rest of today's meetings.

The problem was there was one person standing between Felicia and me—Knight.

It was as if he felt my eyes studying the broad length of his shoulders. He turned. But unlike last night, the soft smile wasn't there.

I saw hard lines around his eyes. Obsidian irises glaring at me. His sexy jaw fixed.

I didn't know whether to turn and run, but instinct kicked in. A mafia queen doesn't run. I slowly let my gaze drift to the doorway. Kimble was scanning the crowd. He always was.

I held my ground, throwing my shoulders back, jutting my breasts forward. I removed the glove from my left hand to offer it to Felicia. I continued to make my approach. As I moved closer, Knight blocked my next movement. He wouldn't let me in the receiving line.

"We need to talk," he hissed.

"I'm here to offer my sympathies to your mother and your sister," I whispered, desperately trying not to make a scene.

"No." He gritted his teeth. "You're coming with me."

I squeezed my eyes tightly. "Knight, this isn't the place."

"I'm making it the place. I insist."

I thought I was quicker than him, but he wound his hand through mine. My body reacted to the contact when it shouldn't have. He tugged me away from the line. Kimble instantly reached inside his jacket. I put my hand up to stop him from following us.

I wasn't familiar with the maze of back offices in the church. Knight shoved open a door. I realized it was one of the confessional rooms. He locked the dark mahogany door behind us. It smelled like incense and velvet. The wall was lit with red votive candles.

"Why didn't you say anything?" he growled.

"This isn't the place to discuss business." I realized my mistake when his eyes clouded with venom and fury. We should be kneeling. Praying. Begging for forgiveness in this room.

"Business?" he huffed.

"Look, Knight. You've been gone a long time." He wasn't the first angry organization member I'd had to settle, but he was the first one that made me want to beg to erase the last five years of our lives. To undo the hurt. To lace it back together like it was never ripped.

I kept my voice steady. "We could set up a meeting once you've had a chance to finalize all of the funeral plans and events. I'll give you as much time as you need." Forty-eight hours was ungenerous. I could extend the grace period.

His hand extended toward me, and my breath caught. I didn't know if he was going to grab me and pull me toward him or strike me. The fire in his eyes was a mix of hate and lust. Instead, he turned with little space to move in the confessional.

"You are going to give me time?" he mocked me.

I nodded. "Whatever you need. Really. I remember how hard it was when my father died." I didn't mention that he never contacted me. My father died from complications from pneumonia only a year after Knight was shipped to

Paris. I had stared at my phone for weeks, hoping, praying, begging he would reach out to me.

"I had a meeting with Paul last night," he explained. "I know everything, Kennedy. I know what you own. Who you have deals with. What you stole from my family."

"I've stolen nothing."

He shook his head. "Who are you? What happened to that girl I met?"

I sighed. "The girl in the pool house?"

"Yes." His eyes softened briefly. "Why are they calling you the queen of the Crescent City? How the fuck did that happen?"

"You make it sound like a bad thing." My eyes narrowed. He had no idea how hard I worked to earn the respect of our fathers' peers.

"You're proud of it?"

I shook my head. "You grew up mafia royalty. Don't judge me."

"But this? How?"

I started to realize he had been kept in the dark. Raphael hadn't told Knight anything about our arrangements. I was as shocked as he was.

"You could have stayed in touch," I whispered.

"I stayed away because—" He shook his head. "It doesn't matter. You need to understand something. I'm taking it all back. Every damn thing you wrenched away from my family."

"Knight, it's business. You know that."

"Don't!" he yelled. The growl in his voice echoed around the small chamber. The candles on the wall shook. I expected Kimble to rush in, but the confessional was soundproof. "You don't get to lecture me about business,

140

About families. About organizations. About deals and negotiations, you knew nothing about. You were a college grad lounging at the pool. Drinking on Instagram. What the hell, Kennedy?"

I slid the glove over my right hand, taking my time to make sure my fingers fit securely. I'd met with impatience and rage for years.

I met his eyes.

"Trust me, I'm not the girl who drinks on Instagram anymore." I stepped closer so he could hear my whispers. I inhaled his cologne. His masculine scent that I'd dreamed about almost every night since he left. Nights I'd shot straight up in bed, wishing I could get on a plane to Paris. I wanted to hear his voice. I wanted to look in his eyes. I wanted to see his sexy grin and laugh with him about something utterly ridiculous. This version of Knight was foreign to me. He was angry. Bitter. Soulless.

"That's fucking clear," he spat.

I unlocked the latch. "Have Paul call Renee. She'll set up a meeting for our legal teams." I closed the door and walked into the hall.

Kimble instinctively wrapped an arm around me as soon as I appeared. My knees shook, and my palms were sweaty inside the gloves. I believed I had masked it all from Knight.

"We're leaving now," he stated.

I nodded my head. "Okay." I couldn't argue. I had to get as far away from Knight as I could.

CHAPTER 18
KNIGHT

TWELVE HOURS EARLIER

Paul looked as if he had aged like a president in the five years I'd been gone. His hair was gone from the top, and there were heavy lines around his eyes. Deep crevices from stress. Lines that developed from the dark secrets he kept for my family. I knew the man had been working around the clock since my father died, but it was more than black circles under his eyes.

"We need to move quickly," I stated. "Dad always wanted me to run the organization from here once I moved from Paris. Are there papers to sign? Just put them here." I tapped the top of my father's desk. I was impatient. I was unsteady from running into Kennedy.

I reached for the crystal decanter on the corner of the desk. I poured a rich bourbon. I wasn't going to let it register that I was the man sitting behind the desk now.

"Knight, we have a lot to discuss about your father's estate." I saw the weariness blanket him.

"Is there a question about the will?" I asked. "A dispute? I thought that was rock solid."

"No. nothing like that. You are the sole heir with specific requests on behalf of your mother and Seraphina. There are notes to set up a trust to keep the Castilles from receiving anything."

"Of course," I muttered. Family had boundaries.

"Is it the off-shore accounts?"

He sighed. "I think I should start with these." He shoved a file across the desk. I opened the top flap.

"What the hell is this?" I saw the ledgers. The numbers. The property listings. "This is the warehouse district. And the distillery." I glared at Paul.

"There are more." He handed me a second file thicker than the first.

I shook my head. "I don't understand. There are second mortgages. Third mortgages. Losses. On every single fucking property." I skimmed the notes. "What organization is this? Who does my dad owe this money to?" I gulped the bourbon, trying to decide what was fact or fiction. "Is this a real company?"

Paul crossed his leg over his knee. "It's very real."

"Carpe Noctem, LLC?" I closed my eyes as the pain of a knife sliding between my ribs might feel. "It's not possible. It can't be." I shook my head.

"It's Kennedy Martin. You should know she has notes like this all over town. She owns New Orleans now."

"Kennedy? The girl I dated?"

"She studied furiously under her father before his passing," Paul explained. "He taught her his own techniques. They've worked for her."

"What the actual fuck, Paul?"

"She's fair. Respected. But she's not backing down or going away. She's made a mark here. Most of the organizations like doing business with her."

"Why?" I was fucking dumbfounded.

He shrugged. "A pretty face, but a lethal business mind. It has its draws."

"What do I do? How to get the properties back? I want the distillery."

"You'd have to exceed your projected profits for the next three quarters. She already takes a hefty share of all the revenue."

I ran my hands through my hair. "How did my father allow this to happen? He never mentioned one damn word to me about this."

Paul expected the questions. He was the only one who knew. "He tried to expand in shipping to beat out Lucien Martin. He overspent. He didn't know the market well enough. When things floundered, Kennedy set up a meeting and offered to bail Raphael out."

I blinked. "And he accepted her offer?"

"He did. And more than once. It's been going on for three years. She became his bank. It's all here in the files. She has a hold on almost everything in the Corban Organization."

"Fuck," I muttered, refilling my glass.

Paul cleared his throat. "But there is one corner of the business she doesn't own."

"What is it?"

"Well, Seraphina and Brandon came to your father a few months ago. One of Seraphina's friends wanted a financial backer to start her company. Your father offered to fund it a hundred percent. He is the sole investor."

"Oh shit. Tell me it's not a bridal shop."

"It's not." Paul unclipped his leather binder and retrieved a file. "It's a small tech company."

I felt the pit in my stomach rise to my throat. What was my dad doing in tech?

"This is what I have? A tech company?"

"You still have all the other properties, but you no longer own a majority in any of them. Kennedy Martin does."

"Stop saying her name." I waved my hand in the air.

"Well, most people do call her queen of the Crescent City."

I stared at him. "I didn't need that."

"Sorry. It's been a long few days."

"Why don't you go home? I'll read these, and we'll meet again after the funeral service."

"Yes, sir." Paul rose to his feet.

I was about to correct him. My father was the sir. But he was gone. I was the head of the Corbans. "Good night, Paul. Thank you."

"I'll see you at the church in the morning."

I leaned into the chair, prepared for a moment alone when my mother walked into the study.

"You're done with your meeting."

I looked up from the statement on the tech company. "Yes."

She looked happier. Lighter. She carried a glass of wine with her. "Your father would be pleased to see you sitting there." It wasn't sentimental the way she said it. Just a matter of observation.

"Maybe." I kicked away from the desk and stood. "I thought you had gone to bed."

"I changed my mind." The glass dangled in her hand. I wondered how many she'd had. "It's strange upstairs."

"Oh." I hadn't thought about her sleeping in the room she shared with my father. "Why don't you move across the hall? We could have that taken care of for you tomorrow."

She shuddered. "What? You think I'm afraid of your father's ghost or something?"

I eyed her. My mother, Felicia Corban, an anomaly to all mothers. Graceful and beautiful. But cold and unaffectionate where her children were concerned. Her moods were hard to read. Her thoughts even harder.

"I have no idea. It would be understandable."

"We haven't slept together in years." She sank onto the small loveseat. "We haven't shared a bed, much less a room. Your father's ghost can try to haunt me all the fuck he wants."

She was drunk. I had to listen closely for the way she began to slur the end of her words.

"Mother, why don't I get one of the maids to help you to your room?" I realized I didn't know where that was. I didn't know shit about my family. My parents hadn't shared a room in years? What the fuck? It was bombshell after bombshell tonight. I didn't want to know more. I couldn't.

Maybe the light in all of this was Seraphina. She and Brandon were expecting a baby. They had their own house now and were out from under the Castilles's roof. She was the only sane one left.

"Did Paul tell you about her?" she carried on.

"About who?"

"You know who," she hissed. "That whore you used to follow around with puppy dog eyes."

146

I grimaced. "Kennedy."

"Yes." Her expression changed. Her smile curled like Maleficient's would. "She's the queen now. Taking things. Ruling them. Spitting in the faces of good families. Our families. Our people, Knight."

"I heard." I didn't want to acknowledge much when my mother was like this.

"But she's beautiful. That's what they say. So gorgeous." Her words ran together from the wine. "They just want to fuck her."

"Okay. I need to get you upstairs," I cut her off. There was a button on the desk that would ring for one of the house managers. I pressed it, counting the seconds until someone carted her out of here.

"You still can't have her." Her finger extended in my direction. "You can never have her."

"And why is that?" I took the bait.

"She doesn't think you're good enough for her." My mother shrugged when one of the new servants entered. "Are you, Knight? Are you good enough for the queen? Do you ask yourself that? Is that what you're wondering?"

I shook my head. "Good night. I'll see you at breakfast."

This was a damn nightmare. A family saga, torn from a Greek tragedy.

"Good night." She held onto the man's arm, and I was glad when I couldn't hear her voice any longer.

I took my glass and wandered the grounds of the compound. It was aimless, pointless walking. From outside, things seemed the same as my last visit home. That had been for Seraphina's wedding. The lawn was manicured. The fountains churned. The hedges were in neat rows. It appeared as if nothing had changed. I climbed the stairs to the pool deck. I stared at my reflection in the pool.

I couldn't admit it to anyone. I couldn't utter the words. Or let them see the cracks. Fuck. I wanted to jump in the deep end. Stay under a little too long. Hide under the diving board. Let pain consume my body. Make my lungs burn. My muscles ache. Anything, but to feel what I felt. I didn't want to swim or float. I couldn't keep treading water like this.

I crouched next to the water, skimming the top with my palm.

I walked back into the house and laid out my suit for my father's funeral.

CHAPTER 19
KENNEDY

I t had been a week since Raphael's funeral. In that time, it felt as if another five years had passed. The door opened, and I stepped into the heat. My high heel landing on a pile of crushed gravel. The air conditioning in the car hummed.

"Ms. Martin, we weren't expecting you." The foreman on the high-rise project gripped the blueprints under his arm.

Kimble guided me to the makeshift table where the crew gathered to go over the plans. The bobcats and forklifts made it almost impossible to hear anything they had said before they realized I had snuck up behind them.

I smiled. "Hi, boys. Just checking in on your progress."

Harry Sallow wiped the sweat from his brow. He was the construction manager. "We're making headway."

"Good. Would anyone like to show me around?"

"I can if you'd like," he volunteered.

"Yes. I would like to see what you've done since my last visit."

The shell of the building was constructed. If anyone hadn't noticed the tallest building in New Orleans by now, they weren't paying attention. The hotel was unlike anything the city had seen before. It was dominant. Classy. A beacon for the city.

"Right this way." Harry stepped over a block of concrete and handed me a hard hat.

"Thank you." It fit awkwardly on my head. I didn't have time to adjust the strap before he had jogged into the front entrance.

"As you can see, we have the wiring in for both the lobby and the casino." I approved of the work so far.

He walked around the lower level, pointing out prominent features. "The two restaurants are this way." I followed him through metal barricades and caution tape. "See? It's coming along."

"No electrical work here, though?"

"Not yet."

"Hmm." I glanced at the ceiling. It was monstrous. A giant chandelier was going to hang in this exact spot. "Thank you, Harry."

"Sure thing, Ms. Martin."

We returned to the others, waiting outside of the construction zone.

"We could go in the trailer if you'd like, Ms. Martin," one of the crewmen offered.

"That's okay." I had been in the trailer before. It smelled like stale sweat, old coffee, and tobacco. "Thank you, boys."

I climbed into the car, and Kimble drove me back to the office.

"I need to see Renee this afternoon," I announced from

the back of the SUV. I scrolled through my phone. I didn't have an update from our state lobbyist on the casino rights.

"I'll make sure she's in your office today."

"Thank you."

I stopped when an email popped up on the screen. There was a congressional meeting tonight on Louisiana's gambling statues, specifically the Crescent Towers proposal.

"I can't wait until this afternoon. Take me straight to her office. Now." I had a bad feeling about the alert. We had been working with local and state officials for months.

I sent my attorney a quick text. I hoped she was prepared to give me answers.

"But you can fix this," I pressed. It wasn't often I made office visits. I did the summoning. A lesson my father taught me. Make people come to you.

Renee hesitated. "I'm working on it. I'm as surprised as you are about the special committee hearing tonight."

"I pay you not to be surprised."

She exhaled. "Honestly, I think it's just a formality. You shouldn't have anything to worry about."

"But if I do? If you're wrong? If I don't get the casino permits?" I couldn't sit. Renee's office was near the river. I watched a barge float past, pushing cargo. It wasn't one of my vessels.

Renee was in her early fifties. She had two kids who were both in high school. They both wanted to go to LSU. They were a family of tigers. Her diploma hung on the wall, along with portraits of her children when they were younger.

Renee never worked for my father. I hired her the day after he died. I needed someone I could trust. It came down to her or a man with a rust-colored mustache. I choose Renee. She had been a business and legal force ever since. For something like this to happen, was unusual. Unprecedented.

"Why don't we get some coffee, Kennedy?" she offered. "We could talk through what the committee might do."

Over the past four years, she had also stepped in as a type of surrogate mother. Although, neither of us would admit to categorizing her that way. She was sharp-witted and brilliant, but she was also kind. As long as I paid her well, she kept my secrets. I sometimes looked at the photos of her kids and envied them. They had a mom who was strong and maternal. I didn't know how that worked. How any of it worked in a functioning family.

"No." I shook my head. "I have more meetings. I left the site and rushed here as soon as I had the alert. I don't need the extra stress right now. I can't lose this. If the casino doesn't open, I'm screwed."

Renee rounded her desk and placed a gentle hand on my shoulder. "The casino legislation is going to happen. Patience. Okay?"

Her voice was calming, but my stomach continued to do flips. "Thanks, Renee. Keep me updated every hour."

"All right. Even if the session runs past midnight?" she asked.

"Especially if it does." I rarely slept at night. I would wait for her calls.

"You've got it. Anything else I can do to help?"

I shook my head. "Just get that law passed."

The rest of the day I spent in and out of meetings. By the time I arrived home, all I wanted to do was kick my heels across the room and sip a crisp wine.

Bella greeted me in the kitchen. "You're home so late. You've been working a lot, Ms. Martin."

I managed a smile. "It's part of my responsibilities."

The sun had started to set.

"Can I bring you a cocktail?" she asked.

"Yes. Wine in the pool courtyard, please."

"I'll be out in a few minutes."

I changed into a swimsuit. It was a red one-piece with a deep V that stopped just below my navel. The sides had been strategically cut away. I was hot, and I thought about swimming laps tonight.

I emerged on the pool deck, followed by Bella. She brought a wine chiller as well as a cheese plate.

"Just in case you get hungry."

"Thank you."

I made sure the volume on my phone was turned up. I didn't want to miss Renee's call.

I tasted the wine and leaned back, staring up at a starry sky.

"Carpe noctem?" The growl invaded my ears and rattled my spine. "Your company is carpe fucking noctem? I still can't believe it. I've heard it. Read it. Seen the doc, and I still don't believe it."

I almost shattered the glass at the sound of his voice. My eyes opened.

"How did you get in here?"

Knight grinned. "I just told them who I was at the front

door. I was even given condolences by your butler. Seems my father used to pay you visits here."

"You should go." I swung my legs around, but Knight was there, blocking them. His solid body, an obstacle to any movement I made.

All I could think about was this moment five years ago. Here. Him chasing me down. Kissing my lips.

"I'll call Kimble," I warned.

He huffed. "I'm surprised about a lot of things since I've been back. Keeping him on your payroll is at the top of my list."

"You don't have the right to judge anything I've done while you've been gone."

The look in his eyes said otherwise.

CHAPTER 20
KNIGHT

The suit. She was wearing a red bathing suit. At night. Under the fucking starry sky like a damn siren. Who wears a fucking bathing suit when the sun goes down?

"Kennedy." My jaw clenched. So did my fist and in it the notice I had received from her office. Scrawled across the top in embossed gold were the words *Carpe Noctem, LLC*. "What is this?" I demanded.

Her eyes fell to my fist. It gave me a brief second to scan her breasts. To admire the way the dip between them made my mouth water. She'd always had the most beautiful skin. Skin that should be licked and tasted. Worshipped.

"Oh, I'm sorry." She tried to reach for the paper, but I recoiled. "If that's from my accountant, it's only a routine letter. You can throw it out. We'll set up a new payment plan. I meant to tell him to extend the grace period since, well, since your father..."

My eyes narrowed. "The interest rates on these loans are absurd."

She sighed. "Your father agreed to the terms. He was willing to pay the interest."

"Well, I'm running things differently than he did. I can't agree to this. I'm not going to pay you double what I should."

She shrugged. "The contracts were signed. They aren't renegotiable. No one in their right mind would redistribute that money at a lower interest rate. I have to abide by the original agreement."

"You could tear them up." I tried to keep my eyes on her face, but it didn't rein in my restraint much better than a full view of her legs. I'd always loved her legs. Long legs I had stood between. Kissed. Massaged. Felt the firmness of in my palms.

"But I won't," she answered. How did I shake her? How did I knock logic into her?

I felt the electric charge at the end of my thumb before it even grazed her shoulder. She stared at the end of my hand. Was she daring me to touch her? Begging me? My thumb inched closer. I fought every instinct in my body to keep my hands off her.

The instant my hand clasped around her, the heat surged between us. I'd lied to myself when I'd fucked other women. I said I could forget Kennedy. For years I had let the lie take over. Five years it built in Paris. London. Munich. The lie was layered with women. I never looked in a woman's eyes and felt devotion. Any of them could have been Venus, sprung from the sea—it didn't matter. No one else was Kennedy. There were no emotions with the other women. Nothing and no one came close to what this woman did to me. What she used to do to me.

The letter fell to the pool deck. "Knight." Her voice was soft and sexy. A call to my primal side.

I cupped the side of her cheek. "Don't say another fucking word," I growled as I took her mouth against mine. It was a kiss that had been raging beneath the surface since the night I left New Orleans.

My lips burned for hers in a way I didn't know was possible. I wanted to bruise her. Bite her. Leave a mark from this kiss she would never forget. She drew a ragged breath and tried to push off me, but I wrapped my arms around her, grazing her skin. Digging my fingers into her flesh.

Our tongues tangled as if we were each trying to sear the other one more cruelly. My heart pounded beneath my ribs. I'd opened the gate to a dangerous game. I couldn't undo it. I'd wanted this woman when we met. Nothing had changed what her body did to me. My hand slid along the dip of her lower back until I gripped her ass firmly. She hissed, but the kiss raged on.

How long could we stand next to the pool this way? Groping. Desperate to crawl under each other's skin.

"You hate me," she whispered. I lowered my mouth to her neck. I kissed her throat, following the V the swimsuit made.

"No." I hooked a finger beneath the strap, it was fastened with a figure-eight clasp. "I can't."

"Only five minutes ago..."

I took a full handful of her ass in my palm. "Stop talking." I kissed her roughly. She threw her arms around my neck.

I was drowning. Getting drunk on her lips. When it abruptly halted at the sound of Kennedy's phone. She wrangled herself free and dove on the chaise to grab it.

"I need to take the call. I've been expecting this all day."

"Go ahead," I groaned.

She held the phone to her ear. "Renee? Oh, God, what is it? What happened? Did they vote?"

I rubbed the side of my jaw, watching her walk to the end of the pool where the diving board was perched. I lost the rest of the conversation. I sat at the end of the chair.

Minutes later, she padded over in her bare feet. "I'm sorry, but I have a long night ahead of me."

"Everything all right?" I stood, towering over her.

"No. It's not. But I'll handle it." She smiled. "I always do."

"You won't tell me what it is?" I asked.

"No."

I studied her, wondering where this unfazed version of her had come from. Paul told me she had been trained. But the woman in front of me had instincts. She had confidence and command. I was starting to understand why they called her a queen. It wasn't an exaggeration or an honorary title. She had the kind of fire in her eyes that would put men's head on spikes.

I retrieved the letter we had trampled and shoved it in my pocket. "I'll call my accountant tomorrow," she explained. "I am sorry about the mix up."

"I'll make the payments. I don't agree with the contracts, but money's not an issue. Not with me running the organization now."

"That's good to hear."

Kimble walked into the courtyard. "Do you need me?" he asked.

"Everything's fine. Mr. Corban is leaving. Can you set

up my office, please? Tell Bella I'll need dinner served there tonight. I just have to run upstairs and change."

He nodded, but his eyes were on me. Hounding me like they always did.

"Kimble," she pressed.

"I'll take care of it." He was hesitant to leave us. "The office will be ready."

Kennedy draped a pool towel over her arm. "I'm sorry about this. All of it." She looked up at me.

My fingers grasped her wrist. "Have dinner with me. Tomorrow night?"

"Is it business or pleasure?" she asked.

"Pleasure. Only."

I saw the way her eyes lit. It was only a second, but the flame was there. It was real.

She scrolled through her phone to check her schedule. "Any time after six," she reported.

"I'll pick you up at seven."

"Where are we going?"

I chuckled. "It's a surprise."

"You always liked to surprise me." She grinned.

"Maybe I still do." I walked with her to the foyer.

"Good night."

"Good luck with your crisis," I called to her as she ascended the massive staircase.

By the time I was done with her, Kennedy Martin wouldn't know what hit her.

CHAPTER 21

KENNEDY

I hadn't pulled an all-nighter since college, but that was exactly what happened when Renee called to tell me the sub-committee on gambling legislation wanted to postpone their vote.

I was on the phone with our lobbyist three different times. We scrambled to try to push for an early morning vote. I talked to every big donor I knew. I had to apply pressure. Someone needed to make this vote happen, or I was in jeopardy of losing the Crescent Towers.

I finally climbed into bed at 6am. I plugged my phone into the charger, turned the volume on high in case there were updates from the team, and pulled a sleeping mask over my eyes. The cool satin was soothing.

Six hours later, I awakened. "Shit. Shit. Shit." I threw the mask on the floor. I had missed calls and texts from Renee. I quickly dialed her.

"Where have you been?" she asked.

"Sorry, just tell me. Did they vote? Did we get it?"

"The vote has been postponed indefinitely."

My heart sank. "Indefinitely? That can't be right."

The blinds were closed in my room. Only sunlight filtered at the very edges near the drapes. I felt disoriented. I stood to open the curtains.

"I've got some ears on the ground. I think I know what happened."

"Tell me." I was desperate for answers.

"There's a new lobbyist. He showed up last night. He has a big backer in the tech industry who are swaying Senators Merritt and Hyde. Apparently, a huge PAC was set up in the last few days with enough money to fund both of their re-election campaigns."

"I can fund their re-election campaigns," I argued. This couldn't be happening. "Who is it? Who is the donor?"

"You know how these things go. Shell companies fund the PAC."

"I want to know who it is. I want a name." The landscapers were outside mowing. I turned from the window.

"We'll find out who it is, but it's going to take time. I need a few days, maybe a week."

"Do you have any leads? Anything?" I was grasping at straws.

"All I know is the PAC is called BONO. For the Betterment of New Orleans."

"Doesn't ring a bell." I felt despair. Dread.

"Me, either."

I groaned and plopped on the bed. "Renee," I pleaded. "Don't let this happen to the project."

"I won't. In the meantime, I'll still use our contacts. Our lobbyist is still working. Construction is going well, right?"

"Yes. It's on track."

"That's good. Keeping the project on schedule is key to

pushing the legislators. It's going to come together, Kennedy. You'll see. Focus on those things you can control, and I'll focus on the others." She was one of my only employees who called me by my first name.

"I could go under," I whispered.

"You won't," she urged. "You won't."

I took a giant inhale. "Call me with any updates."

"I always do."

I hung up with Renee. It was after noon, long past when I usually drove to the office. I would work the rest of the day from home. I wandered to my closet. Work from home meant work casual attire. I saw the red swimsuit hanging by the door.

I remembered Knight's visit. The kiss by the pool. I touched my lips lightly, wondering if they appeared blue. Knight had kissed them raw. It was a brutal punishing kiss. It drained logic and sanity from my head. I'd waited five years for that kiss. I could still feel it burning my skin. It made me wonder what he had in store for our date tonight. More than that, I wondered why I agreed to go.

I watched from my bedroom window when Knight pulled into the circle drive. I was hidden by the curtain. He wore a dark suit. Fitted. From this far away, he still looked edible. I took a full inhale. The doorbell rang, but I didn't budge. It wasn't long before Bella knocked on my door.

"Ms. Martin, your guest has arrived," she announced, and I pretended I wasn't aware that the air was twenty degrees warmer since he walked through the front door.

"Thank you, Bella. Tell him I'll be down in a minute." I

was dressed. I stepped into the high black heels that added inches to my height. I hesitated in front of my vanity. I flipped open the marble box and pressed the button underneath the velvet shelf. The tiny door popped, and I retrieved the necklace. It was a bold statement. I touched the pearl against my skin once the clasp was fastened. It was a night for surprises.

I took one step down, and I saw him. I swallowed, wondering if I should call off the date. The man waiting for me at the bottom of the staircase looked like a wolf ready to draw in his prey. Was it the Knight I knew, or was it a new version that had let in more darkness than light?

I took a second step and then a third until my hand was in his.

"You look gorgeous." He leaned to kiss me on the cheek.

"Thank you."

"You ready?" he asked.

"I am." My phone was tucked in my small purse. I had silenced it. "Where are we going?"

"I have a full evening planned. You'll see."

"Marguerite's?" I guessed. I had been to visit her a few times after Knight's move to Paris. She knew I missed him. But eventually, even that became too difficult for me.

He chuckled. "Even better. Trust me."

I expected Knight to drive us out to the bayou. He liked the places on the road less traveled. The anonymity that came with dive bars and local haunts. As we turned through more downtown streets, I had a sinking feeling. It felt off.

He pulled along the curb as the valet hurried to the driver's side of the car.

My eyes cut to him. "Is this a joke?"

"Is there something wrong with the food here? I heard it was the best in the city. Now."

The curly French writing scrawled on the marquee lit behind his head. We had arrived at the Vieux Carre.

When I didn't answer he quieted the music in the car. "Look, it's a little ironic. I thought it would be a good place to start our truce."

"That's the truth?" I questioned.

"It seemed like a good place to start. You can show me around your hotel. But we do have reservations that start in five minutes. I could cancel?"

"No. No." I shook my head.

The door swung open, and the valet's eyes bulged when he realized who I was. "Ms. Martin."

"Good evening." I smiled sweetly.

Knight nodded at me. "I knew we'd have excellent service at least." He offered his hand as I stepped on the curb.

"Ahh, I see. You're here for the service."

He chuckled. "I just want to see where the night takes us."

I felt a lump in my throat. I wasn't sure if this was a date or psychological torture.

I shouldn't have been surprised Knight reserved the private dining room. I often held special meetings here if I needed extreme privacy with the combined services of the hotel.

Starring at the man sitting across from me, I felt as if the night was incredibly fragile. As if we could tip the scales towards pain or happiness with very little energy. The tension was only increasing, and I didn't know how to diffuse what buzzed between us.

"So, tell me. Have the tunnels been useful?" he inquired. It was a loaded invasive question.

My eyes popped. "I thought this was a date, not a business meeting."

He poured our champagne casually. "It is a date. But we have a lot to catch up on. I imagine you've been able to put the passageways to use in five years. No?"

I flatted the linen napkin in my lap. "I don't think it's a good idea to talk about organization business. I was under the impression the truce was about us." I stared at him blankly. "If it's not, I'll have a driver take me home. Crew can set up a meeting with whomever your assistant is. Not that I'm going to talk about the Vieux Carre in that meeting either."

He held his hands in the air in a defensive posture. "It's clear we have a lot to learn about who we are now. I'm sorry."

I finally exhaled. "I'm sorry I jumped down your throat."

He grinned. I felt more at ease.

"Why don't you tell me about Paris?" I suggested. "Not the wineries. Just what did you think about living in France? What was it like? I've never been. Tell me all about it." A safe conversation starter was what we needed.

I listened to Knight's stories about the coffee shops and the museums. He described his flat. He told me how difficult it was to have his piano shipped. It took weeks. He was having the same problem having it brought back to the States. Neither of us allowed a hint of the memory associated with his baby grand.

He spent weekends in London. I was afraid to ask about the women. I knew they existed. Of course, they existed. It was hard to picture him taking trains to Prague or Florence without some gorgeous brunette on his arm. But he never let it slip. He had taken up polo and had a box at one of the football stadiums. He had immersed himself in European culture, picking up Italian and German. I was impressed. We finished the first bottle of champagne.

"It sounds beautiful," I mused. "Especially the French countryside. Did you think about moving there and out of the city?"

"You would love it. Champagne for miles." His sexy smile made me shiver. Or maybe it was the rumble of his voice. "It's a quiet life for sure. I think the countryside is the perfect place when there is no more of this." His eyes made a quick scan of the dining room.

"Work?"

He nodded. "The pace. The race to conquer. Yes, once that's out of your system, then I would move to the French countryside and learn how to make my own champagne."

I wondered if he was asking me how long it would take to eliminate the drive from my system. Was I capable of not wanting projects like Crescent Towers? He knew the Kennedy that would rather read by the pool. He knew the girl who was looking for a way out. The one desperate for freedom.

How did I make the last five years evaporate? How did I go back to that night at Marguerite's? How did I convince a naïve younger me to hop on that plane to Paris and never look back?

Those were my thoughts as I sat inside my empire. An empire I had clawed and fought to build. I surpassed my father's vision. I had triumphed over Raphael. I survived when markets were volatile, and other businesses failed. I adapted and evolved to stay on top. Yet, to have a chance to do it again, would I rather live in the French countryside drinking champagne with a man who made my heart spin?

I heard my phone buzz inside my purse.

"Go ahead," Knight allowed.

"No. We're in the middle of a date. Business can wait."

A few seconds later, the phone buzzed again.

"Someone might need you. I understand. I'll find the server and order more champagne."

I nodded. "All right. I'll be quick. I promise."

He walked out of the room and dug into my bag for the phone. Renee had sent five texts. Damn it. I held my breath. Maybe I couldn't change the past five years when I had a chance to choose Knight. But I could choose him for tonight.

I fired off a quick text to Renee without reading any of her messages.

I'll call you tomorrow. I'm not available now.

I hit send, feeling satisfied. And feeling like I had taken the first step to reclaim what my life could have been.

CHAPTER 22
KNIGHT

I handed the server a hundred-dollar bill. "Deliver the bottle to the suite," I instructed him. I wanted him to by-pass our table for part two of the date. We had almost finished dinner. Dessert was also going to be served upstairs.

"Yes, sir." He hurried to the bar for the bucket of champagne.

I was about to enter the dining room when my phone vibrated. It was Seraphina.

"Hi," I answered. I had a few minutes to give Kennedy.

"Knight, where are you?" She sounded out of breath.

"I'm out. Everything okay?"

"Yes. No. I need to talk to you. Are you at the office? Can I meet you there?" she asked.

"Slow down." I sat on a velvet bench nearby. "I'm not at the office. Can you tell me now?"

"It's not something I can tell you over the phone," she pleaded.

I rubbed the back of my head. "I'm at dinner. You're going to have to wait until tomorrow."

"Are you with Kennedy?"

"Why would you ask that?"

"Never mind. Can we meet at the stables tomorrow? After breakfast?"

I had a meeting with Paul first thing, but then I was free. "I'll see you there. Are you okay until then? Are you sure?"

"Yes. Yes. I'm fine. I'll meet you tomorrow. Enjoy your date."

I scowled. "I didn't say I was on a date."

Seraphina hung up before I could say anything else. I tucked my phone back in my pocket. Kennedy was sitting at the table when I returned. She was looking across the room.

God, I wanted to know what was running through that gorgeous head of hers. She had grown more beautiful in five years than I could have imagined. I wondered if she had chosen the dress and the necklace to fuck with me. I swore it was the same black cocktail dress she had worn when we met. I slid the door closed. She turned.

"Where's the champagne?" She saw I was empty-handed.

"I have a second surprise for you."

Her emerald eyes widened. "And what's that?"

"I sold my apartment when I moved to Paris. I haven't been back long enough to buy something new. I will soon."

"Oh? I assumed you'd move into the compound."

My jaw tightened. "With my mother? No thank you. She can keep the manse." She wandered the halls after midnight, carrying empty wine glasses, shouting at the servants for refills. She was a drunken banshee.

"I guess she would be a challenging housemate."

I chuckled. "That's putting it mildly. Anyway, our date is moving locations."

"Now are we going to Marguerite's?"

"No. Trust me. You'll like this better."

Kennedy rose from the table. "Should I keep guessing?"

"No, you should not."

She stepped into my space. "Fine."

Her lotion was the same citrus scent. It entered my nose, filling me with memories. Fuck. The compulsion to kiss her was strong. I gazed at her pink lips. I repressed the urge and offered her my arm.

"Let's go."

Once we were out of the dining room, we turned the corner for the elevator bay. Kennedy kept glancing at me. She expected an answer. She knew her way around the hotel. This wasn't a backway to the parking garage. I inserted an antique brass key into the control panel. It clicked softly with the flick of my wrist.

"Upstairs?" She blinked. "Part two is upstairs?"

"What's the difference between going to the suite and back to my place?"

I thought it was a valid point.

She faltered. "The people in this hotel work for me. I've never gone to a room with a guest. That's a huge difference."

Did it make me a dick that I was glad to hear that? Somehow it was minimal validation that Kennedy hadn't been with another man. Absurd conclusion, but I wanted that truth. I wanted her untouched. Unloved. I wanted her free to be mine.

The bell dinged, and the doors retracted.

"You can put on an offended act for the staff that you don't want to go upstairs with me." I saw the goosebumps on her flesh when I whispered in her ear. "Or you can do what you and I both know you want. Step in the elevator."

Her eyes flashed to mine. "I don't take orders from anyone," she hissed. "I haven't for a long time. I no longer have to submit."

My hand curled around her wrist. I pressed my fingers into her tender skin. "You could change that for one night, couldn't you?" I winked. I thought she was going to slap me, but she wrenched her hand free and marched into the elevator.

"Are you coming?" She eyed me.

Without saying a word, I joined her, turning the key inside the elevator.

I HAD PLANNED strawberries dipped in chocolate. A second bottle of expensive champagne. I had planned filling the original claw-foot tub with scalding water. Bubbles. Candles. Roses. Pulling out all the stops. But every fucking plan went out the window when we walked in that suite.

The door closed, and the world became ours.

Kennedy spun and I took her mouth with a sensuous kiss. Long. Slow. Her mouth opened. A quiet moan escaped from her throat. My tongue probed, remembering how her tongue liked to tangle with mine. I pinned her against the wall, savoring the taste of her. The beauty of her. I nipped behind her ear, trailing her throat back to her mouth. The kiss was deeper this time. More punishing. Brutal. But who was the predator and who was the prey?

My fingers dug into her shoulders, rotating her toward the wall. Her palms slapped against the hand-painted wallpaper as I began to drag her dress to her hips. Her skin was covered in goosebumps. I grinned. My mouth covered her ear, the side of her neck, the softness of her shoulders.

"Knight," she rasped.

I felt the heat between us. The undeniable chemistry that always raged when I was near Kennedy. My fingers dug into her exquisite curves. She mewed, and I wondered if it was possible to end up on my knees before I even carried her to the bed.

She did things to me. Unspeakable monstrous things. She'd haunted my dreams. Plagued me with promises of what could have been. Another life. A richer life. A complete life with nights that ended in fucking each other senseless.

Tonight could drown out the mistakes of the past. I would make sure it did. There would be no question tomorrow when we awakened that we had burned something permanent on each other's souls.

CHAPTER 23
KENNEDY

Midnight. That was the color of his gaze. I saw deep midnight eyes when I tried to sleep at night. Those lashes. His strong jaw. The way he used to say my name with a growl. Five years of fantasy were unraveling in this moment. Five years of imagining when and how we'd finally be able to fan the ember that smoldered between us. It had never been extinguished. If this wasn't proof of that, I didn't know what was.

Knight's powerful frame held me close to the wall while his hands had free reign of my body.

I turned my head, catching his lips. It was a blistering kiss. Hot. Possessive. I gulped for air when his hand slid between my body and the wall. God, what had he done to my dress? Was it on or off? I only felt the strong magnets under my skin pulling him closer, harder. Did we have any control over what happened next?

His hand flattened against my navel as it made a slow purposeful descent. He took his time, imprinting the memory on my skin. I hissed when he slid farther, prying my heat open. Seeking my clit to torture and please.

My knees quaked, but Knight wrapped his hands to my chest, yanking the cocktail dress out of his way. He wanted access to my entire body. My nipples were bare for his fingers to take, pluck, squeeze. He was possessive and determined.

I reached behind me, running my fingers into his hair, drawing his mouth to the crook where my shoulder met my neck. He sucked my skin. Licked and lavished it.

His finger slipped inside me, followed by another. I whimpered and heard the approval reverberate in his chest. I was soaking wet. But he knew that the instant he touched me. He plunged another finger in my entrance until I felt stretched and filled. My mouth opened to protest, but he covered it with his.

He began pumping inside. Rubbing my nipples. Kissing me. It was as if the first lick of a flame started in my core and began to pour through my limbs. I raged with burning heat. The orgasm blazed while I panted and begged. I didn't know what I was begging for. I didn't know if I was forming words or only making sounds.

But Knight spun me in his arms and scooped me against his chest. He carried me through the suite into the bedroom. Our eyes met, and I wondered if he was thinking the same things I was. Would this erase the pain? Would this be the start of something new? Or was this just tonight?

He lowered me to the bed. He worked the zipper on the side of the dress and peeled it off my body.

"Much better," He grinned, admiring my body. He continued to undress me until I was practically panting.

"What about you?" I teased.

"You want to play? That's fine. But me first." I was speechless. He left me no room to argue.

I wanted to touch him. To see his clothes hit the floor in a pile. I didn't want anything between us any longer. We'd come close before, but this was a new chapter. A new beginning for our bodies. I reached for him, ready to snap every button on his shirt with a click of my fingers, but he knelt before me. Knight Fucking Corban dropped to his knees.

The hunger in his eyes. Oh my God. I gasped, taking in the full scope of what he was about to offer me. Did I need five breaths? Ten? How did I prepare for what was about to happen?

His palm flattened on my stomach. I watched every move. Every touch. I trembled.

"Shh." His eyes had turned darker than coal. They never left mine as his head began to dip. Lower. One kiss on the inside of my thigh. He dipped lower. Another kiss. Our contact didn't break until the first lash of his tongue.

"Oh shit." My head reeled back. My eyes closed and I lost the battle.

His tongue was nothing short of greedy. Dragging back and forth, lapping, sucking. I arched into his mouth, demanding my own reward. He grunted bursts of satisfaction.

I clawed at the bed. Thrashed trying to find gravity. I loved where his mouth was. Right where I wanted it. Fucking my entrance, claiming it with a cascade of kisses.

I was falling into an abyss. Knight's eyes. His mouth. His fingers canvassing my body with strokes of heat. I wanted to swim in it as long as the waves would carry me. And they didn't disappoint. One slow roll after another, crashing and crashing. My body hummed and sang until I was a heap of panting exhaustion.

I dared to open my eyes as he rose from the floor. He unbuckled his dress pants and they fell to the floor. I watched in awe as his clothes fell away and I finally was able to take in all of him. More than a glimpse of a sculpted bicep, or the ridges of his abs. He revealed he had snagged condom from his pocket. Alright, he was prepared, at least.

He climbed on the bed, one knee at a time, crawling toward me as I felt my mouth go dry at the sight of him. *All* of him. Holy hell. His cock sprang toward me. I'd felt the smooth length of him in my palm once. But never did I imagine his full cock was this powerful. This damn intimidating.

"You okay?" He waggled his eyebrows, inching closer.

I nodded, wanting to feel the weight of his body pressed into mine. Needing his skin to sear mine. I wanted the friction and the sweat. I wanted to wake up smelling like him and still feel the bruises from our bodies rubbing together.

The masculine scent rolled off him. He crushed my mouth. It was a kiss that tasted like sex and champagne. I moaned when he urged my legs wider. I clawed at his shoulders. Big strong arms that I'd wanted in my bed, now they were like pillars of muscle anchoring me to the mattress. I needed them now to brace for what was undoubtedly the most anticipated sexual experience of my life.

"Five years." He broke away, licking my throat.

I moaned, arching my back, offering myself to him. "I know." It was hard to speak.

Everything about our past had been hot, consuming,

electric. I never pretended he didn't leave a mark on me. I just wasn't able to admit it to anyone. For the first time in years I was with him the way I had imagined it would be. I wondered what the mark would be this time. Would I survive it?

He nudged himself at my entrance. I sighed before the blistering friction began. He gave me seconds to adjust to his width. To recover from his massive shaft. It wasn't possible. Knight's cock was the stuff dreams were made of.

"Five years I've waited to do this," he growled as he thrust inside me. Shit. He wasn't the only one who had waited. He filled me, stretching, taking possession, claiming me as his. It felt fucking incredible. The fullness of him stole my breath.

Our eyes locked as the thrusts began slowly at first, then changed pace. My hips ground to meet his. The frenzy built. Our mouths crashed together. Our tongues lashed as Knight pumped in and out of me. The speed changed. Long slow movements as he sank deeper.

I whimpered at the intensity. I clung to him.

He cupped my breast as another kiss made my head spin. His hand canvassed my body until he was able to create a wedge enough to rake his fingers over my clit. The strokes rattled me. Broke me.

Bursts of noise sputtered from my throat. I came apart in his arms. Strong, loving arms.

"Fuck," he grunted, giving in to his orgasm to match mine. "You're mine, Kennedy. Finally," he groaned in my ear.

I nodded. I would have agreed with anything, but that sentiment had always been true. I was Knight's a long time before he ever took me to bed.

"Say it," he growled. "I want to hear it."

"I'm yours," I whispered. "Yours."

The climax swept through me. My veins were coated in glitter. My skin was dewey. My lips were swollen.

With a final grunt, Knight hilted himself inside me so deep I screamed toward the ceiling. He rooted himself as if this was home. As if our bodies were finally together. The crystals on the chandelier rattled and I felt the satisfaction down to my toes.

Knight nipped at my lips. His eyes sparkled with mischief. God, I loved seeing him happy.

"Hey, you." He grinned.

"Hey," I murmured softly. Was he glowing like I was? Did men do that? It sure as hell looked like it from this angle. I touched the side of his brow. He was drenched in sweat.

"Want to try out that tub in there?"

"That means we have to move." I pouted. "I don't think it's possible." The weight of him made it hard to breathe, but I didn't want to budge. This felt good.

He chuckled. "You don't have to move. I'll do all the lifting for you."

Before I knew what he was doing, Knight had collected me from the bed and strolled through the bathroom door. He kicked it open.

"See?"

I laughed. My arms draped around his neck. "This could be the start of something very complicated, you know that? We both have a lot at stake."

"Like what?"

He lowered my feet to the floor. "Like business." There was nothing else more important to either of us than continuing our legacies for our families. He was lying if he tried to convince me otherwise.

He spun the handles on the tub. It began to fill. The idea of soaking in the tub was soothing. Our bodies were sore. I wanted to soak until my fingers were pruned, and the water was tepid.

"It's only as complicated as we make it," he responded. "This isn't about business."

I considered his answer. We had missed the middle, but maybe we were still the beginning and the end. Maybe Knight was right. We didn't have to make it complicated.

I couldn't imagine either of us was willing to walk away from what we had just unleashed.

CHAPTER 24
KNIGHT

I used to sleep in. Those were the mornings that followed nights of endless drinking and partying. Now I set my alarm for 5:30, so I could run or fit in a trip to the gym before going to the office. It was my new routine in Paris. One I adopted after turning thirty. It seemed more significant than New Year's resolutions or bucket lists. Just get up and fucking run.

This morning I made an exception. I awakened with Kennedy in my arms. Her skin was warm. Her lips were pink. Her body was fucking incredible. After last night, it was mine. She was mine. She always should have been. I was too scared and stupid five years ago to do what I should have done.

We'd be ruling the city together now. She'd be my queen. Mine.

I grinned, thinking of what we had forged in this bed. We were bonded. Bound together. We had fused our bodies into one, and it was not like anything I'd known. Kennedy wasn't like other women I'd known.

She stirred, sliding her torso over my chest. God damn when her nipples brushed over my ribs, my cock ached. It was hard in five seconds, growing longer. Screaming at me to take her. She smiled lazily when she realized I was watching her.

"Good morning."

"Good morning." I gripped her hips, drawing the rest of her on top of me. I wanted her to know just how damn wild her body drove me.

"Ohh," she whispered, sliding over my dick. The warmth of her body drove me insane.

I hissed as her hips moved back and forth. She was wet. My fingers dug into her waist, urging her to rock. Farther until I was inside her. I wanted her sweet pussy, bare. Just a taste. Just a second.

Kennedy pressed off my chest, tilting her hips and I thrust upward. We both groaned at the intensity. Skin on skin. She plucked her nipples as the sunlight streamed through the windows. I hadn't bothered to close the blackout drapes last night.

"Fuck me," I commanded as she began to ride faster. Her mouth parting with pants and coos. "That's it."

But I didn't know how long I could last watching her fuck me this way. I wrapped my hands around her waist, and with a quick maneuver, planted her on her stomach.

"Knight," she hissed at me. I had ruined her perfect rhythm. I'd reward her in time for making the sacrifice.

I kissed behind her ear, as I caressed and massaged her ass. She began to wiggle and shake her hips as I raised her ass higher in the air. I groped her cheeks, squeezing them roughly.

"Shit," she murmured. "That feels good."

I grinned as I positioned myself behind her. Her head whipped to the side.

"I love fucking you, Kennedy," I growled.

My cock slammed into her with a powerful thrust and Kennedy yelped. Her hands quickly reaching for the headboard. There was no holding back. I pounded against her flesh. I pumped in and out. She threw her hips back, matching each thrust with one of her own.

"Yes," she cried as we lost our damn minds. "Don't. You. Stop," she demanded as I watched her disappear into an orgasm. The way her body succumbed to her ecstasy was something to watch. The trembling began to take over. I was going to come like this if I didn't slow down. The condoms were in my pocket on the floor. Shit. I couldn't pull away. Not while she was coming on my cock. Squeezing it. Coating it with heat and pleasure.

I pumped in and out. Sliding against her tight pussy walls. Fuck. Me.

She glanced over her shoulder, sucking on her lip, watching me take her from behind. My chest tightened at the same time the base of my spine began to sing with electrical pulses. The instinct to bury everything I had inside her was hard to fight.

One gush before I was able to pull out. I groaned, fisting my shaft as I came on her back. Kennedy panted, slowing from the orgasm. Our bodies stilled. Our breathing was heavy.

"Don't move. I'll grab a towel." I hopped off the side of the bed and returned. She hadn't changed positions.

"Thanks," she whispered as I cleaned her back. I followed the lines of her hips. I cupped her gorgeous ass.

"Damn, Kennedy. Your body..." I didn't even know how to finish that sentence.

She rolled on her back, rolling her wrists back and forth. "Thank you?"

I chuckled, tossing the towel across the room. I crawled back on the bed to join her.

I kissed along her neck and throat. Her eyes closed and she smiled, soaking in the attention I gave every inch of her body.

"Do you think we should talk about it?" I asked.

Her eyes flew open. "About what?"

"This. Us." I pressed up on my elbow. I wanted to be able to take her all in and to follow her expression

"We've done something we've waited five years to do."

"I-I—" I caught her lips between mine and aligned my body to hers.

"Don't overthink it," I teased, pulling her to my chest. Her skin was warm and soft. I grazed the contours of her nipples and hips.

She purred at my touches. "Knight?"

"Mmm?" I wanted to lie in bed with her all day. Get to know her again. Memorize all the sounds she could make and the movements of her body.

"Never mind. You're right. I'm just going to overthink it. I'll screw it up if I try to talk about it. This was perfect and beautiful. The entire night with you was the most incredible experience..." Her voice began to crack.

I nodded, making another row of kisses along her collarbone. "It was perfect." I leaned up on my elbow. "You can't screw it up. Not when it's like this. I couldn't have asked for it to be more or anything else."

Her eyes softened with recognition. "You're right.

Again. But don't get used to that," she teased. "I prefer to be the one who is always right."

I laughed. "I may have waited five years for you to say that. And it was damn worth it."

"Really?"

"Want to say it again and see what happens?"

Her fingers lingered next to my jaw, just enough I could feel the heat from her palm. The anticipation of her touch drove me crazy. Everything about her drove me crazy. It always had from the first night we met in the pool house, to the first-time laying eyes on her after five years. She was a part of me and always had been since the first hello.

Loving Kennedy. Needing Kennedy. Wanting Kennedy. The desires and passions for her had felt like dreams suffocated under water and now they'd been freed to the surface. They were floating, buoyed by the truth that we no longer had to hide our feelings. Kennedy was my shelter. She was home. She was everything I'd always wanted. She was mine after all this time. The woman I loved was mine.

"I need to know something."

I tilted her chin so I could look in her eyes. "What is it?"

"Just tell me you won't go back to France. You won't leave again."

My eyes widened. There was a deep pain in the center of my chest. "No. Oh my God. No. I'm here and staying here. You know why I had to stay away and you know why I'm back."

I searched her eyes for belief in my words. For reassurance that she trusted me.

She blinked back tears that had begun to dampen her lashes. "It was a stupid thing to say."

"It wasn't." I kissed her lips. My mouth covered hers. "I won't leave again. I promise you."

She moaned lightly as I stroked her tongue with mine. She curled her naked body around mine. I pulled her under me, the kiss becoming more fevered with each lash, with each bite until her hips began to dance wildly. I slipped my fingers inside her warm center.

"Ohh," she moaned as I began to pump them in and out, taking time to swirl around her clit and touch so that each and every nerve-ending was on fire.

She stared into my eyes with a look of wonder and question.

"Shh." I pressed a rough kiss on her mouth. "Just come again."

My fingers worked their magic against her sensitive bud, lavishing her swollen pussy with gentle and fierce strokes until she began to unravel in my arms once again.

Her nails dug into my shoulders. She arched away from me as I pressed into her. She quivered relentlessly gasping for air and release, riding out the orgasm in giant waves.

There was nothing sexier. Nothing hotter. Nothing more erotic than holding Kennedy while she came.

I kissed the corners of her mouth. "I promise I won't leave again. I swear to you."

She nodded, smiling. "I believe you." She bit her lower lip. "You think you can fuck me now? Please," she begged with a gaspiness in her voice. "Promise me with your soul."

The words hit me hard and I knew exactly what she meant and what she needed.

I realized how swollen my cock was. Her orgasm had turned me on. The total focus and attention on her experience had been erotic as hell. Her legs wrapped around my waist, and I eased my cock into her. There were no words. No sparring threats. No teasing. It was her body and mine, melting into one. I pumped in and out, in slow indulgent thrusts. My fingers tangled through hers, sealing our palms together.

"Don't leave me. Ever," she whispered.

"Never." I tasted her throat and the side of her neck.

The match had been lit again. The embers stoked as I slid my cock in and out. Over and over. If I began to speed up, Kennedy grabbed my ass to slow me down. We both wanted it to last. To linger. We wanted to cling to time, to each other, to this bed and the sheets until we could barely breathe. I had one condom left and it seemed like it was a mile away lodged in my pants from last night.

"Kennedy," I moaned, knowing I had to break apart for an instant.

She whimpered. "Get it." She could read my mind. The quicker I completed this task the sooner I'd be buried inside her.

We felt the pain of the space and the coolness of the air as our bodies tore apart. I lunged to the floor and dug through the pockets until I found the second condom I had slipped in my pants last night. I rolled it on and climbed back on the bed.

She smiled as I moved toward her like a lion. Although, we both knew she would never be anyone's prey. She arched her back, inviting me to take her again. There was something so raw and primal between us. I settled between her legs and slammed into her, shattering both of us with the fervor of my thrust. She moaned and I pumped inside her, feeling her warmth wrap around me. Seconds apart had awakened our appetites. It was as if we needed to relive last night all over again. I fucked her wildly and she fucked in return with the same hunger. We would slow only to hasten the pace again and then rock back to the fullness, the intensity we had always wanted to drown in.

Her eyes locked on mine and our rhythm became the same undulating wave ready to crest and surge. Crash together. Shatter together. Fall apart in each other's arms.

She said my name over and over. I kissed her. Our bodies shook and swept us out to sea with orgasms that would have shipwrecked anything in their paths.

I felt dizzy and soothed. More alive. More in love.

We fell asleep in a tangled embrace.

"What time is it?" Kennedy asked.

I wasn't sure how long our morning post-sex nap had lasted.

"I'm not sure. Early? Who the hell knows?" I wanted to pounce on her again. I felt giddy like I was seventeen. I was never going to get enough of her. I knew now it wasn't possible.

She pushed forward. "I need to check my voicemails. I had messages last night I ignored. I have a legal meeting today. I can't stay in bed. Renee's expecting me." Her hair was a mess. She looked gorgeous.

"What kind of legal meetings?" I pried.

"It's about a casino I'm building. I've run into legislative issues."

The giddy feeling sank into a pit. Fuck. I wasn't going to admit what I had done. It was business. I had to rebuild everything my father lost. I had to restore the fortune.

Reclaim our name. We were New Orleans royalty. Everything I did for the organization was to protect the Corban legacy. For now, that secret was safe. I was sorry that she wasn't going to get what she wanted this time. I couldn't let the Crescent Towers project happen.

"Let's skip everything we planned. Order room service. Drive to the beach. Whatever we can do to ignore real life."

She laughed. "Funny. I run a multi-billion-dollar organization. I don't have days off. Hand me my phone? If I don't check in with Kimble in the next few minutes he will freak out and show up with a gun pointed at your face."

"He always points a gun at my face."

She shrugged. "True. It's his job."

"Are you going to tell me why out of all the security options you kept that guy around?"

"I'm still alive." Her stare was hard. "That should be enough for you to know."

"Fair enough." Maybe later she would tell me about the things that had happened while I was gone.

I strolled to the foyer table and walked back through the suite with her phone.

"We are going to have breakfast." I eyed her.

"I need my phone."

"Breakfast?"

She sighed. "Yes, breakfast." She smiled slyly.

I handed her her purse and walked to the bathroom while she checked in with her bodyguard. I brushed my teeth and started the shower.

I cracked the door. "Join me?"

She nodded. The phone was pressed to her ear. "Just a few more minutes," she mouthed.

"I'll start without you." I winked, closing the door so

the steam could collect inside.

I stepped inside the shower. The water felt good. So did the bath last night. We had talked for hours. Had tub sex. More sex. Talked again until we fell asleep.

I lathered the soap between my palms. I kept watching the door, waiting for Kennedy. I thought I heard the outside door slam. I turned off the water and grabbed a towel.

I stepped from the glass enclosure and wrapped the towel around my waist. "Kennedy, what's taking so long?"

I stared at the bed. It was empty. I wandered to the kitchen. She wasn't in the suite. I spotted the brass key on the table by the front door. Next to it was the necklace. I lifted it in the air. The diamonds sparkled around the pearl. The inscription swung back and forth. *Carpe Noctem*. We had done that last night. More than once.

There was a note scribbled on the hotel stationery, pinned to the hotel latch on the door. What was going on? I yanked it off the lock.

I KNOW IT'S YOU. You're BONO.

THAT WAS ALL IT SAID. I clasped the pearl in my hand. Shit. How did she find out? Paul had combined a shell company on top of shell company to protect the PAC's identity.

The water from the shower puddled at my feet. I closed my eyes. She wasn't coming back to the suite. That note might as well have been a death threat. She was going to come after me with everything she had.

I had to be ready.

I needed a plan to get her back.

Also by Violet Paige

Royal Romance

Tempting the Crown

Risking the Crown

Loving the Crown

Protecting the Crown

Resisting the Crown

Cold Love Hockey Series

Cold As Puck

Cold As Ice

Cold As Hell

Mafia Romance

Her Mafia King

His Mafia Queen

Their Mafia Empire

Football Romance

Turn Over

Sidelined

Dirty Play

Double Score

Billionaire Romance

Not Husband Material

KEEP IN TOUCH WITH VIOLET

Click here to sign up for my newsletter.
(P.S. You will ONLY receive information about *me, me, me*)

Follow me on Instagram for everything social.

Follow me on BookBub!

Stay connected with Violet's Vixens
http://www.thevioletpaige.com
authorvioletpaige@gmail.com

Made in the USA
Columbia, SC
29 April 2023